Half Baked
Schemes

Mary M. O'Donnell

Annie's®
AnniesFiction.com

Books in the Chocolate Shoppe Mysteries series

Library of Congress-in-Publication Data
Half Baked Schemes / by Mary M. O'Donnell
p. cm.
I. Title
2017951053

AnniesFiction.com
(800) 282-6643
Chocolate Shoppe Mysteries™
Series Creator: Shari Lohner
Series Editors: Janice Tate, Ken Tate
Cover Illustrator: Bonnie Leick

10 11 12 13 14 | Printed in China | 9 8 7 6 5 4 3 2

In her excitement, Jillian Green didn't know what to do first. She looked at the smartphone she still held in her hand, her finger poised over the speed-dial button for her grandmother's number. But she hesitated. Surely it would be better to deliver the good news in person.

She was alone at the family business, The Chocolate Shoppe Bakery, located on the town square of Moss Hollow, Georgia. It was closing time, and she had just locked the front door of the bakery when the phone call came through. She sprang into action, counting out the cash register, boxing up the remainders from the glass-front bakery case, tidying up the customer area, and washing up the last few things in the kitchen so it would be ready for the next morning's bake. Luckily, when she stopped at the bank to drop off the day's proceeds, the teller seemed preoccupied and didn't make the usual inquiry about the health of Jillian's grandmother and great-aunt or want to commiserate about the hot summer weather.

Even so, when all her tasks were finished, it was nearly an hour before Jillian was on the road to Belle Haven, the Greek revival mansion she called home. Once the heart of a plantation, the mansion was now surrounded by just ten acres that, according to stipulations in the deed, could only be passed from family member to family member or else be donated to the town of Moss Hollow.

After a twenty-year absence—during which time she lived in California and had a career in advertising—Jillian lived with her grandmother, Bertie Harper, and Bertie's twin sister, Cornelia Montgomery. It was the goal of the three women that Belle Haven should remain in the family. They didn't want to be the ones who "let down" their ancestors by losing ownership of the home that had been in their family for over two hundred years. That's why the phone call was so important. It was another step toward being able to keep the property in family hands not just for the present, but well into the future.

She drove a little faster than she should have, and it wasn't long before she pulled into the long driveway. Bypassing the offshoot that made a loop in front of the house, she went straight through the porte cochere at one side of it to park in the garage located in the back.

Inside the house, she hurried from room to room looking for Bertie and Cornelia, calling out their names. She knocked on Bertie's master suite bedroom door, but got no reply. Not finding them on the first floor, she took two steps at a time up the circular stairs, which were lit from above during daylight hours through a round, stained glass dome, to reach the second floor. Her aunt Cornelia's bedroom door was open, and the room was unoccupied. She walked to the steps that led to the third floor. They were covered with a fine film of dust from lack of use. No one had been up there for weeks.

Possum, the cream-color cat with chocolate-brown accents who had taken up residence with them, greeted Jillian by winding his body around her ankles.

She leaned down to run her hand across his back. "Where are they, Possum?" She straightened up, then trotted back down the steps to head outside. She took a crushed-gravel path that led to what had once been a tobacco-drying barn, now in the process of being converted into a venue for events to be catered by The Chocolate Shoppe.

They had rented out the mansion for several special occasions, including a couple of weddings, a one-hundredth birthday party, a fiftieth wedding anniversary, and even as a set for a low-budget horror film. But as large as Belle Haven was, the arrangement of the rooms wasn't really designed to suit an "upscale event" as promised in the brochure. It was Bertie who had added that detail at the last minute without approval from Jillian, and now she was frantically scrambling to meet the promise in the brochure. There had once been a ballroom in the mansion, but, sometime in the past, it had been divided up into smaller rooms, perhaps when modern indoor plumbing was added, Jillian thought. She considered the ballroom a loss, but it would be difficult to try to return the house to its original state now, even if she could.

So, besides working to refurbish the huge mansion—deep-cleaning, painting, and updating decor—they had been throwing every cent they could spare to make the old barn into a place where a really large group of people could gather. Whereas Belle Haven was classically elegant, the barn was rustic with elegant touches—at least it would be when it was completely renovated. It would be a while before they reached that point. The basic electrical and plumbing were in place throughout the building, but the only things available in the planned professional-grade kitchen so far were the sink and a dishwasher, which Cornelia had gotten a deal on. The heating and air-conditioning had been installed, as well as the restrooms, and the large, open main area with its new and polished wood floor was completed. As it was now, it would be just enough to be used for its intended purpose.

As she approached the building, she sighed. Landscaping still needed to be done. Aunt Cornelia, with help from the garden club and a couple of local men who hired out as gardeners, had made great progress in the back acreage. No longer jungle-like in appearance, it was on its way to becoming like the impressive garden it must have been in the distant past. *But these things take time*, Jillian thought. The fencerow along the edge of the property was still overgrown, with trees and woody vines intertwined with the fencing. It was impossible to mow there, so the grass and weeds had grown tall over the summer months. She hoped it wouldn't put off her prospective client.

She opened a side door to the barn to hear Bertie and Cornelia exchanging heated words.

"We are not going to have any of your wacky group here to—"

"They're not wacky! I've told you, they're paranormal investigators." Cornelia enunciated each syllable of the last two words as if she were speaking to someone who didn't understand the language. "It's all very scientific."

"My aunt Fanny," said Bertie. "They'll come over here with their useless devices in that van of theirs, emblazoned with 'Ghostbusters' or whatever it is, and word will get out that we're some kind of loopy lunatics, more than it already has."

Jillian watched Cornelia press her lips into a straight line, a sure sign she was about to respond with words that would be better left unspoken. To prevent an escalation of their disagreement, she cleared her throat and charged forward, practically slamming the door shut behind her to get their attention. She tried to keep her voice light, as if she had heard nothing of their conversation. "Bertie! Aunt Cornelia! I've been looking for you everywhere. I have some great news."

Both looked at Jillian, Bertie with her right eyebrow raised and Cornelia with her left, but neither said anything.

"This is the part where you say, 'Tell us your wonderful news, Jillian!'"

Bertie sighed. Her voice was deadpan. "All right. Tell us, honored granddaughter, your wonderful news so that we may share in your delight."

Cornelia gave her sister a disdainful look. "See? That sarcastic tone of yours is just the sort of thing that drains the enthusiasm out of everything that makes life interesting." She looked at Jillian. "Go ahead, dear. I'm listening."

This atmosphere of discord was not ideal for delivering her news, but there was no getting around it now. Maybe a different subject would help ease the tension. "I got a phone call from Patricia Smith. She's going to be here on Friday to see if the barn will work as a set for an episode of the baking show she's producing for TV."

Her news was met with slightly puzzled stares.

"Remember? I told you several months ago that I was going to contact her when I saw an announcement about it in that trade magazine we get at the bakery. Besides that, I'm sure you must have seen the ads that were placed in some of the national cooking magazines that we take, asking nonprofessional bakers to apply to be contestants on *The All-American Baking Contest*. They've already chosen bakers from each state to compete for a place in the finale, and they'll be changing locales for each episode. Apparently, the place they had lined up for the Deep South region had to cancel at the last minute, so they need another location quick."

The sisters exchanged a look that Jillian couldn't read.

"Bertie, it's *the* Patricia Smith—you know, of *Blissful Baking* fame. We have a copy of her cookbook in the kitchen that you've had as long as I can remember, and we have a copy at the bakery too. You know the recipes from that book like verses from the Bible. Aren't you even a little bit excited?"

Ever practical, Bertie looked around the empty room and then at Cornelia. "Is there any chance of this place being ready for something like that?"

Cornelia had been acting as the general contractor for the project, organizing carpenters, plumbers, and electricians. When Cornelia had volunteered, Jillian had been hesitant at first to let her take on the responsibility, but with the bakery and the other events that had been held at the mansion, it was the only choice.

She and Bertie were just too busy. Despite her reservations, Jillian had to admit that Cornelia had done the job well.

Cornelia shook her head. "I'm sorry, Jillian, but the kitchen is nowhere near ready. And the rest of the appliances are going to be pricey. We just can't afford to buy those right now."

"But that's the beauty of this. The kitchen doesn't have to be completely ready. The show will provide all the equipment, tools, and ingredients that the bakers will need. All we have to supply is the space—this room. And besides getting paid, we'll get national exposure. It's a level of advertising we couldn't begin to afford. This could really put The Chocolate Shoppe on the map."

Jillian turned to look around the room. Windows had been added to let in daylight, and some temporary lighting had been strung across the exposed rafters, but there were only wires sticking out of the walls and ceiling where sconces and chandeliers were yet to be placed. "Do you think Mr. Hepplewhite could install the lighting before Friday?"

Cornelia looked doubtful. "I don't know. I'll call him."

Before Cornelia had become their contractor, she disdained the use of a smartphone. Now she was never without one. She reached in her pocket, pulled out her phone, and began tapping the screen. In a few seconds she was conversing with the electrician.

While Cornelia was on the phone, Jillian spoke to Bertie in lowered tones. "This really is a great opportunity, Bertie."

"I know it is." Bertie closed her eyes. "I'm just starting to feel stretched a little thin."

Jillian, a good three inches taller than her grandmother, put her arm around Bertie's shoulders. "Please, Bertie, whenever you feel that way, let me know. That's why I'm here, to help share the load. Why don't you take off work tomorrow? You can just stay here all day and have a mini vacation."

"As if I'd be able to relax with Cornelia raising a fuss. I'd rather be at the bakery than listen to her go on and on. At least Lenora has some sense." Lenora Ryan had worked alongside Bertie at the bakery for years, and had been a friend of the family even longer.

Jillian hadn't wanted to bring up the subject of their disagreement, but since Bertie had raised the subject, she might as well ask. "What do you mean about Cornelia raising a fuss?"

Bertie rolled her eyes. "She's decided we've stirred up a ghost or something out here. She called it a poltergeist. Said she's been hearing unexplained noises, and heaven knows what else. You know how she is. She wants to bring in those so-called 'investigator' friends of hers. She's being ridiculous as usual."

Jillian tried to remain a bit less critical than Bertie, even though she was in basic agreement with her. "Maybe we can put her off and she'll forget about it now that we're looking at a deadline to have this part of the barn ready."

"Or she'll dig in her heels and say it has to be done now for the safety of potential renters. Stubborn old woman." Bertie shook her head as if those words described only her sister. But then her expression changed. She seemed to remember something and actually looked a little sheepish. "There is something else." She reached into her pocket, pulled out an envelope, and handed it to Jillian. "This came today. It was originally postmarked two weeks ago. It must have been misdelivered and then sent all the way back to the post office in Augusta before it finally got here. It's from our cousin, Genevieve. She's asked us to take care of her five-year-old great-granddaughter for a week or so while the girl's parents are getting ready to move out of state."

Jillian shook her head as she pulled the letter from the envelope. "We can't do that, Bertie. None of us have the time to chase after a little one." She silently read the letter, its cursive script legible, but a bit shaky.

Dear Bertie and Cornelia,

I'm writing to ask a favor. My granddaughter Lilith and her husband, Mark, are preparing to move to Washington state, and during the last week of August, they need someone to look after their daughter, Bonnie, who just turned five. I would do it if I could, but I've gotten too old, and since I'm in assisted living now, it's just impossible. My daughter Margaret and her husband, Charles, are going to be away on a long-planned vacation during that time, and Mark's parents, the Truebloods, live in Arizona, so you two are the nearest relatives. I have such fond memories of staying with your parents when I was Bonnie's age, and those later times when I stayed with you when you were young girls and I was a young woman. We had so much fun together. I'd love for my Bonnie to have a chance to stay at Belle Haven too before she moves far away.

There was a bit more to the letter, but Jillian had read enough at the moment to know it couldn't possibly work out. "Bertie, that's next week already, and if we can convince Patricia Smith that the barn will work for the TV show, it'll overlap the time they want to film here. We can't look after a child then."

"Jillian, we have to do this. This is family. Being fourteen years older than us, Genevieve used to come and stay here with Cornelia and me when Mother and Father went away on trips. She was like an older sister to us. Your aunt and I have already discussed this and she agrees with me. We have to help out."

Jillian glanced back at Cornelia, who was still on the phone talking animatedly to Mr. Hepplewhite. She looked back at Bertie, who had fixed her with a determined gaze. Even as she wondered how on earth they would possibly manage, she heard herself say, "Okay, Bertie. We'll do our best."

What else could she do? It was her against two stubborn, elderly women.

"Well, we couldn't keep calling it 'the barn,' so when Mrs. Smith was here this morning I said the first thing that came into my head," Jillian said as she walked up the stairs to the second floor of Belle Haven.

Her best friend, Savannah Cantrell, was following her. "So what did you call it?"

"Belle Haven Hall. I hope that doesn't sound too stuffy."

"Sounds okay to me. What did she think of the actual 'hall' then?"

"She loved the interior. It really does look great since the wood floor is finished and Mr. Hepplewhite got the lighting installed. She seemed to be a little put off by the state of the garden, but I told her we could add some mature plants in strategic places, so if they film carefully, it should look all right. I think she's in a tight spot since the other place pulled out at practically the last minute. And I have to say, she loved Moss Hollow itself. They're going to include a snippet about the town and The Chocolate Shoppe too, so we'll get double the exposure."

"So when are these TV people showing up?"

"Mrs. Smith will come next Wednesday with the crew to set up everything in the barn—I mean, the hall. I need to get used to calling it that. And then the contestants are supposed to arrive the next day. We'll have the contestants, the director, the two judges, and Mrs. Smith all staying here at Belle Haven, and the rest of the crew will stay at the Southern Peach Inn. Mrs. Smith had already called to make sure they had enough rooms available, so that's all set."

"What's she like? My mom used to watch her when she had that baking program on TV. I think my grandma probably did too. How old is she anyway?"

"I think she might be a little bit younger than Bertie and Aunt Cornelia, but not by much. I checked the copyright date on the copy of *Blissful Baking* we have in the kitchen. It was published in 1969. She seemed nice enough. A little brusque maybe, but that might just be a difference in her New England manner compared to a Southerner's. Or maybe she's just used to keeping things moving on a TV set."

They had reached the stairs that went up to the third floor.

Savannah looked at the dusty steps. "We should've brought the dust mop up here. This is getting pretty bad."

"I know. I've asked Mrs. Fleming to come in two days next week, instead of the normal one, to help get everything spiffed-up before the TV people arrive. I've added cleaning these steps, the third-floor hallway, and that little bedroom up there to her list since there aren't enough bedrooms for everyone on the second floor." Jillian started up the steps. "I really need to be doing other things besides looking for toys in the attic, but we're meeting Bonnie and her mom on Sunday, so we have to find something to keep her entertained while she's here."

"Is that why you canceled the Sweetie Pies meeting?"

Both Jillian and Savannah—along with Cornelia, Bertie, Lenora, and several other ladies from Moss Hollow—were members of the Southern Sweetie Pies, a baking club that met each Sunday afternoon at The Chocolate Shoppe to trade recipes and taste test each other's baked creations.

"Yes. Bertie called Bonnie's mom, Lilith, and we're going to meet her at noon at a restaurant that's located about halfway between us and have lunch together. Lilith said she was just bringing a suitcase with Bonnie's clothes and one stuffed animal. The rest of her toys are already packed up for the move. Apparently, Lilith's husband, Mark, is going to drive the moving truck they've rented and Lilith will follow him in one of their cars. Then, after they've unpacked, Lilith will fly back to Georgia to get their other car and drive back to Washington state with Bonnie."

"Wow. That's a lot of driving. I can see why they want to spare Bonnie all that."

"Yeah, me too. So I guess it's a good thing, even if I was reluctant to do it. Thanks, by the way, for volunteering to help me out today."

"You're most welcome. I wish I could do more, but I've got a couple of clients who are being audited, so this upcoming week is going to be busy for me too. How are you going to handle looking after a five-year-old on top of everything else?"

"I really don't know how it's all going to work out. I'll just have to take one day at a time. Bertie asked Stacy, our old front girl at the bakery, if she could work a few hours next week. She called back and said her mother-in-law volunteered to look after the baby, so with Lenora and Maggie, and Celia coming in after school, the bakery should be covered."

"Why don't you hire a babysitter for Bonnie? Or you could ask some of the Sweetie Pies. I know they'd be glad to help out."

"That's exactly what I said to Bertie, but she won't have it. She said it has to be family. She promised Genevieve, and I'm the only one who can handle it right now. Cornelia's up to her eyeballs with getting the barn—the hall—and the garden ready, and Bertie will cover the bakery, so I can be here to take care of anything concerned with the TV show. But, to tell you the truth, I'm really starting to think there is more to this than meets the eye."

"What do you mean?"

"Just the way that Bertie is insisting that I have to be the one to look after Bonnie. You know how she's not above mentioning that I'm not getting any younger."

"And that Hunter Greyson is the most eligible bachelor in Moss Hollow."

"Yes, that too. It's no secret that she thinks our local mortician is a catch, and that I'm the one who should catch him."

"So you think she's putting you through a test run for matrimony and motherhood?"

"I wouldn't put it past her."

Jillian had reached a door on the third floor that creaked from disuse when she opened it. Swatting away a cobweb, she reached inside to flip the light switch, which made a loud click. The large area had the same fixtures and switch that had been installed when the mansion was wired for electricity in the early 1930s. Even with the overhead lights on, the room was gloomy, in spite of the three dormer windows along one side. The walls were wood laths without a layer of plaster over them, and the timbers in the roof overhead were exposed. The large room wasn't air-conditioned, so it was hot.

The family always referred to this space as "the attic room," and it was so full of old things that Jillian couldn't even begin to know what all was stored there even though she'd been in it a few times since she had returned to Belle Haven. The room had been a forbidden area when she was little—she supposed Bertie thought it too dangerous, not to mention too dusty, for a child to play in—and she hadn't been interested when she was a teenager.

Her cursory glance took in a battered armoire, several tables of different sizes, mismatched wooden chairs, a telescope on a tripod, some old milk cans, and even a wooden airplane propeller. The propeller was a complete mystery. She wondered what had happened to the rest of the plane and who among her illustrious forebears might have flown an airplane. She sighed, thinking how much more there was to learn about her Belle family ancestry, if only she had the time.

She stepped inside, shivering in spite of the heat. "Well, I always thought that if I were to start believing in ghosts, this would be the room that could do it. But Bertie says this is where the old toys are, so I guess we don't have a choice."

"I'm glad I dressed grungy for this," said Savannah. "Are we looking for something in particular or just any toys we come across?"

"It's both actually. I remember a child-size table set I used to play at when I was little and came to visit Bertie. The table was white, and it had four different-color chairs with it—red, green, blue, and yellow. Bertie used gingham in matching colors to make quilted pads with ruffles for the chairs. And there was a little tea set too. Bertie would make tea with lots of milk in it and mini scones served with peach jam for me. I loved it." Jillian looked around. "She said the table and chairs were up here somewhere."

Savannah sneezed and then reached in her pocket for a handkerchief. "Good thing I came prepared." She blew her nose. "I'm going to see if I can open a window or two, and then I'll see what odd treasures I can find, since you have some idea of what you're looking for."

It didn't take long for Jillian to locate the table and chairs, which were dusty but otherwise in good condition. A taped box was on the table, and Jillian used the small utility knife she had brought with her to open it. She was pleased to see that the tea set was inside and would be fine with just a wash, but was disappointed that the quilted chair pads weren't with it.

From the corner of her eye, she saw Savannah shift a couple of milk cans and a few chairs to get to one window. After it was opened, she turned and disappeared into the clutter around her, then lifted up a canvas sheet. "Come and see what I found."

"Just a sec." Jillian stepped over some things she had moved in order to get to where Savannah stood. Perched on a low bench was a very old dollhouse. It was obviously a miniature Belle Haven. Like the mansion, it had three floors and three dormers across the top of the roof. It had the same number of porch-to-roof columns lined up across the front, supporting the second-floor balcony that ran across the front of the house. "Let's take it out in the hallway so we can see it better."

After much maneuvering, they managed to carry the heavy structure into the bright hallway. There they inspected the back of the dollhouse, which was open for easy access to the rooms. Jillian was impressed that it included a central circular staircase that mimicked Belle Haven's.

"Well, it must have been a pretty thing when it was new, but it sure has seen better days," said Savannah as she dusted her hands on her jeans.

The house was made of wood that looked rough and gray with age, and the roof and one side showed water damage. The siding must have been painted yellow and the columns white at some time in the past, the same as the full-size Belle Haven, but now only a few specks of the paint remained. On the inner walls it was evident there had been multiple layers of paint in different colors.

"I wonder if that's lead paint," said Savannah.

"Wouldn't be surprised. It might be a blessing that most of the paint is gone. We'll just have to sand off any paint that's loose and then paint over it to make it safe."

"Do you think it's salvageable?"

"I think it could be with a little elbow grease."

"Looks like a lot of work to me," said Savannah. She rapped the roof panel that had water marks with her knuckles, making a dull thud. "I think some of this wood might be nearly rotten. It must be really old. Have you ever seen it before?"

"No. Bertie must have thought it was too much work to fix it up for me to play with."

"And just think how many years ago *that* was."

Jillian lightly swatted her friend's arm. "Hey, in case you've forgotten, we're the same age."

"We may have been in the same class at school, but remember, I am three months younger. That has to count for something." Savannah tilted her head to look at the dollhouse again. "Shame. It really does have character, and obviously whoever built it was trying to mimic Belle Haven."

"If I can find someone to take care of the water-damaged parts, I could paint it myself." She paused a moment, thinking. "I wonder if Burton Puckett would be able to fix it. I know he's handy with woodworking, and since he retired from the hardware store, he might have the time. I think I'll call him later. Then maybe Bonnie and I could decorate it. I wonder if there's any furniture for it."

Savannah smiled. "Is this for Bonnie to play with, or for you?"

Jillian grinned. "It could be for both." She headed back into the attic room.

It was a while later when Jillian closed the door to the attic and turned to look at the things she and Savannah had found, which, besides the dollhouse, table, chairs, and tea set, included various antique wooden toys—a set of blocks, a doll bed, a spinning top, an open carriage with two horses attached with leather straps, and a set of zoo animals such as a zebra, a tiger, a hippopotamus, an elephant, and a giraffe. But they hadn't found any furniture for the dollhouse.

"Good thing Mrs. Fleming hasn't cleaned this hallway yet. You'd have to do it all over again with all this dust," said Savannah.

"I'm thinking it might be a good thing to just clean these up here before we carry them down to the living room. I rearranged it a little so there's play area behind the sofa by the windows. We can put most of the toys there, but I think we should just put the dollhouse in the library for now. I'm disappointed about not finding any furniture for it, so far."

"Why don't you try looking at The Dusty Magnolia downtown?" said Savannah. "With all the antiques in that shop, it wouldn't surprise me if Mrs. Toombs has dollhouse furniture too."

"I don't know. Might be pricey. But it's worth a look. I might stop by there tomorrow."

"What's in that?" asked Savannah. She pointed to a small wooden crate with faded lettering on the sides.

"Oh, wait till you see. This is neat." Jillian stepped around the little table to the crate, removed its lid, and then lifted a yellowed newspaper to reveal some books. She picked up one. "Took me a couple minutes to pry off the lid, but it was worth it. I've never seen these before. The top two are old children's books, so I hope the rest are as well."

She showed Savannah the cover of the book in her hand. It had gold lettering and the image of a little girl in a black dress looking up at some birds flying past white clouds. "This is *A Little Princess* by Frances Hodgson Burnett. I loved that story when I was a girl." She placed the newspaper on the table and reached down to grab another book. "This one is *Grimm's Fairy Tales*." She put down the first book and took in the ornate cover of the second, which said the book was edited by Frances Jenkins Olcott and illustrated by Rie Cramer. Jillian flipped to the table of contents. "Oh, this is perfect. It has 'Rapunzel,' and 'Hansel and Gretel,' and 'Little Snow-White,' and . . ." She stopped to count and turned the page to count some more. "There are over fifty stories here. This should help keep Bonnie entertained. I hope she likes to be read to."

Savannah picked up the newspaper and began reading out loud from the masthead on the front page. "*The Times*, London,

Friday, June 15, 1928." She scanned the articles. "It says here that the House of Commons rejected a proposed revision to the *Book of Common Prayer* by a vote of 266 to 220, and the House of Lords debated the Equal Franchise Act which would lower the voting age for women from thirty to twenty-one." She looked up at Jillian. "Do you think these books could have been up here since 1928?"

"It's entirely possible in this place. A shame, though. I wonder why they are up here instead of being in the library. I would have loved these when I was a kid. But if someone put the crate up here in 1928, Bertie and Cornelia might not have known it was even here, or what was in it, since that was before they were born. I guess when you've lived in the family home your whole life, as Bertie has, you don't always bother to investigate every single thing that's been left behind by previous generations."

Savannah reached over to pick up another book from the crate. "Hey, this one's *The Tale of Peter Rabbit* by Beatrix Potter." She gently turned the pages. "Such sweet illustrations. I'll bet Bonnie will love this. Well, I'd say this discovery is 'the bomb,' as we used to say back in the day."

Jillian groaned. "I haven't heard that one used in years. I think I'll stick with the timeless 'neat.' So, shall we get this lot cleaned up and then carried downstairs? I'm thinking that pizza and a chick flick are in order for this evening. That is, if you're free."

"I am. I have a date tomorrow night with James, but pizza and a movie sounds like fun for tonight." James had been Jillian's boyfriend in high school, but that ship had sailed years ago. Now it appeared that something romantic might be developing between Savannah and James, but Savannah would only admit to being good friends. "What about you? Don't you have a date with Hunter this weekend?"

Jillian smiled, a bit of scarlet tinting her cheeks. "Well, yes I do. It's tomorrow night as well. So tonight will be girls' night in. I was just thinking, instead of a romantic movie, how would you feel about watching *The Little Princess*? It's based on Burnett's book, and Aunt Cornelia has a DVD set with all of Shirley Temple's movies."

"You know, I have never watched a Shirley Temple movie."

"You're kidding."

"Nope. I've seen a few clips online, but never sat down to watch one through." Savannah looked down at her clothes. "If we're going to do this, I'd like to run home to shower and change when we're finished cleaning these things."

"I agree—a shower is definitely called for after this. Tell you what, we'll make it a double feature and watch *Heidi* too. That's another classic. So when you come back, bring your pj's and we'll have a slumber party."

"Aren't we a bit old for that?"

"Maybe. Or maybe not. Can't hurt to reconnect with our inner child now and then. We'll make popcorn and watch movies like we used to in high school."

Savannah laughed. "Sounds like fun. I'm in."

After getting rags and a couple small buckets of water, Jillian and Savannah proceeded to dust and wash each item as needed. They had to freshen the water a couple of times before they were finished.

Jillian was delighted as she removed and dusted the books from the crate. In addition to the ones she'd already looked at, she found *Aesop's Fables*, *Peter Pan in Kensington Gardens*, as well as *The Story of the Treasure Seekers* by E. Nesbit, and *At the Back of the North Wind* by George MacDonald. All the books had copyright dates from the 1920s or earlier, and each was beautifully illustrated.

Jillian picked up the last two books from the bottom of the case. "Hmm. These are different. This one is *Mrs. Beeton's Book of Household Management*." She flipped through the pages.

"There are several recipes in here. I wonder if they're any good." She set it aside to look at the second one, which was a booklet with a butter-yellow softcover featuring a drawing of a woman with a 1920s bob hairstyle and wearing an apron. The woman was standing at a table stirring batter in a bowl with various ingredients placed around it, including a bag labeled *Brooke Flour.*

Jillian looked inside the book. "This booklet is from Brooke Flour Mill Company in Great Britain and has recipes for cake and pastry flours. I think I'll show this and the *Mrs. Beeton* book to Bertie later. Who knows? There might be some great recipes in here that we could use at the bakery."

She looked up to see that Savannah was not really paying attention to anything she had said because she was concentrating on cleaning the intricate carving of the carriage and horses with an old toothbrush.

Jillian went back to work, cleaning the crate so she could put the books back inside to carry downstairs. *I wonder why these were put away in the attic instead of being placed in the library,* she thought. *There must be a story here, but now there's probably no one who remembers it. I guess I'll never know.*

Sunday morning found Jillian driving her white Prius down the highway with Bertie in the front passenger seat and Cornelia in the back. Normally they all would have been at church, but there wasn't enough time to attend and still meet Lilith and Bonnie for lunch.

Things had become tense between the sisters again after Cornelia announced that morning that she had arranged for her friends, the Lowlands Paranormal Investigators, to come to survey the barn with their instruments on Tuesday.

Although the conversation had ended before they got in the car, Cornelia must have been going over it in her mind. "As if I need your permission," she muttered under her breath, just loud enough for Jillian to hear. Jillian shot a sideways glance at her grandmother, wondering if Bertie had also heard. Her expression was stoic. It would be just like Bertie to ignore it. *This is going to be a long drive*, thought Jillian. She turned on some easy-listening music to soothe the atmosphere.

She thought some light conversation might help. "When Burton picked up the dollhouse yesterday, he said he'd try to have it repaired and back to Belle Haven by Tuesday or Wednesday. He even said he could paint it by then too, so I told him to go ahead. I offered to pay him, but he refused. Did you know that dollhouse was in the attic?"

Bertie answered. "I did know, but had forgotten about it. It's been up there for years. I don't know who built it, but I seem to remember that it was stored in one of the outbuildings way back and that's why it looks so bad. I think I remember Dad saying it was my grandfather who brought it in and put it in the attic with the intention of fixing it up someday, but he never got around to it, and there it stayed."

"Do you know if there was any furniture to go with it? I looked at some dollhouse furniture at Dusty Magnolia, but it was all so expensive that I decided to pass on it. And then, when I went to the variety store to pick up a couple of coloring books and some crayons for Bonnie, I looked to see if they might carry some dollhouse furniture, but no luck."

"I imagine that whatever furniture there might have been is long gone. But there might be some doll furniture in the room where we store the old clothing. Mother had a lovely dollhouse from her side of the family that she used to let us play with if we were careful."

Cornelia spoke up. "Don't you remember? When we were teenagers Mother gave that dollhouse and furniture to the historical society in the town where she grew up. It was an heirloom, and I think she wanted to make sure it was preserved and displayed so everyone could enjoy it, instead of it being put away in the attic and forgotten about."

"Well, that's a bust," said Jillian. "Anyway, I thought you said all the old toys were in the attic room."

"No, just the old wooden toys, and I knew that I had put that table and chairs in there after you got too big for them. But I wouldn't put anything made with fabric or plastic in there. There should be a box of dolls and dress-up clothes in the storage room with all the old clothing."

"I should have thought of looking in there. Did you keep the quilted pads you made for chairs?"

"I think so."

"Maybe I can look around after Bonnie goes to bed tonight."

"Where are you putting her?"

"Well, I was thinking of having her sleep in that smallest bedroom on the second floor, but with the TV people coming we're going to need it for one of them, so I set up a cot in my room."

Jillian glanced sideways again to see a satisfied smile on Bertie's face. She looked in the rearview mirror at Cornelia to see a similar look on her face. She decided to ignore those smiles.

"I found a crate with some old children's books in it too. Do you know why they were in there instead of the library?"

"I don't recall any books being up there," said Bertie. "Do you, Cornelia?"

"I don't, but there were a lot of years I wasn't living at Belle Haven, so I have no idea what you might have done."

There was just enough edge to the tone of her voice that Jillian broke in before Bertie could respond. "There was a newspaper on top of the books from 1928, so it could have been placed there before you two were even born."

"That's possible," said Bertie. "I always thought when I took over running the house from Mother that I would go through all the rooms on the third floor and get everything organized, but there always seemed to be something else that needed to be done. And it seems unlikely I'll be doing anything about it at this stage of my life. I guess it will be up to you."

"Maybe it's something we can work on together—one of these days, when things settle down."

Bertie turned her head toward the window. "Of course. One of these days."

Once they were just a few miles out, Jillian used her car's GPS system to lead her to the restaurant Lilith had chosen. It turned out to be a charming little Italian eatery, with white linen tablecloths on the tables and a dark-green cloth napkin folded into a tent shape in the center of each place setting. They had arranged to meet around twelve thirty, but Bonnie and Lilith had not yet arrived, so Jillian requested a round table with five chairs, one with a booster seat.

After the hostess had seated them, Cornelia said, "Oh, I forgot my purse." She looked at Jillian. "Would you run out to the car and get it for me, dear?"

"Of course. I'll be right back." She sent a nervous glance toward Bertie and Cornelia, hoping they wouldn't bicker while she was gone. But she was pretty sure it would be all right. Sometimes just a look between the twins was all that was needed to communicate. At least that was quiet, and she knew they would behave once Lilith and Bonnie arrived. They would consider it to be impolite to carry on in front of anyone other than Jillian, even if the other people were also family.

As she walked to the car, Jillian tried to mentally figure out which rank of cousins she and Lilith were. Genevieve's mother, and Bertie and Cornelia's father had been sister and brother, so that made them first cousins. That would make Jillian's and Lilith's mothers second cousins. Or was it first cousins once removed? Jillian quickly gave up. They were family. That was sufficient.

She retrieved Cornelia's purse from the car and had just locked it again when she saw a dark-blue sedan pull into a nearby parking space. The driver was a blonde woman, slightly younger than Jillian, but Jillian thought she had definite features from the Belle side of the family.

When the woman got out of the car, Jillian stepped nearer. "Lilith?"

The woman smiled and approached her. "Yes. You must be Jillian." The two women hugged. "I'm so glad to finally meet you. I've heard so much about you when I've visited Belle Haven with my mother and grandmother."

"So you've been to Belle Haven before?"

"Oh yes. Several times. But it's been a while ago now. The last time I was there was before Bonnie was born. We should've worked in a visit before now, but you know how it is. The first time I visited, I was already in my twenties. Since Dad was in the Navy and was stationed all over the world, I never had a chance when I was a child. So this will be Bonnie's first time to see Belle Haven, but I've told her all about it. And I tried to tell her as much of the family history as I could remember, which I'm afraid isn't much. I'm so glad that she'll have the opportunity to have a visit before we move." She grasped Jillian's hands. "Thank you so much for helping us out."

"You're welcome. I'm glad that we can do it." Jillian felt slightly guilty remembering her initial reaction to the request. "Bertie and Aunt Cornelia are already inside."

"Oh, I didn't know they were coming too. That's wonderful. It will be nice to see them again." Lilith looked at the car behind her. "Bonnie nodded off on the way here. She was so excited last night, I think she barely slept. I'd better see if I can wake her."

Lilith opened the back door where Jillian could see there was a child buckled into a car seat. Lilith spoke soft words and gently rubbed the little girl's hand. Her head moved, her eyes fluttered open, and the little girl began to speak at once to her mother, her sweet voice trilling.

Lilith unbuckled the seat belt and helped Bonnie climb out of the car.

Jillian caught her breath. She didn't think she'd ever seen such a beautiful child. Her still sleepy eyes were the striking blue color of sapphires, her long black hair was so dark it seemed to shimmer like a peacock feather in the sunlight, and her cheeks were a rosy pink.

The little girl was dressed in a white peasant-style top with a wide, lace-edged ruffle around the neck and a cornflower-blue polka-dotted skirt with a large bow at the front waist. She carefully smoothed her skirt and straightened the bow before approaching Jillian with her mother.

"Bonnie, I'd like you to meet our cousin, Miss Jillian Green," said Lilith.

She looked at her mother who nodded, and then, as if she'd been practicing, she reached out her hand to Jillian. "I'm pleased to meet you, Miss Jillian."

Jillian knelt down on one knee on the pavement in front of the little girl so that they would be closer to eye level and shook the proffered hand. "I'm pleased to meet you too, Bonnie."

Bonnie surveyed Jillian's face a moment and then reached out to take a lock of Jillian's long red hair in small, gentle fingers. Her saucer-shaped eyes looked at it with wonder, and then she looked into Jillian's bright-green eyes. "Oh, Miss Jillian, you are so beautiful. I wish I had hair just like yours." Tears welled up in the little girl's eyes.

Afraid the little girl was about to cry, Jillian took a lock of Bonnie's hair in her own hand. "You know, I always wanted to have hair just the same color as yours." It was the truth. As a child she had imagined herself as a Native American princess, with long, straight, black hair, instead of curly red hair that tended toward frizziness in the humid climate of Georgia. It was only kept under control now by the regular application of multiple hair products.

The girl looked puzzled. "Really?"

"Yes, really. At school, I was often teased—they called me

names like copper-top and carrot-head, and one boy even called me fire extinguisher."

Bonnie let go of Jillian's hair and folded her arms. "Well, he wasn't very nice, was he?"

Jillian laughed. "I didn't think so. But then, I might have been a bit oversensitive too."

"What's that mean?"

"Oh. That's when your feelings get hurt too easily."

"You mean like when I get upset and Grandmamma tells me, 'Sticks and stones may break my bones, but words can never hurt me'?"

"Yes, something like that."

"But words do hurt sometimes, don't they?"

Jillian nodded. "I have to admit that, yes, sometimes they do."

"So how do you know if you're oversen . . . oversen . . ."

"Oversensitive."

"Oversens'tive or not?"

This was turning out to be a deeper conversation than Jillian had expected. "Well, I suppose if you spend all your time only caring about what other people think about you, you might be oversensitive."

"You mean like Snow White's wicked stepmother always asking the magic mirror who was the fairest in the land?"

"I never thought of her that way, but you might be right."

"She was bad though."

"Yes she was."

"But you're not. I can tell. So, you can be oversens'tive and be good or bad?"

"I guess so."

"Are you still oversens'tive?"

"Sometimes, I suppose I am." Before the child could ask another question, Jillian decided to be proactive. "Say, are you hungry?

I think we should go inside and meet your other cousins, Bertie and Cornelia. Then we can have something to eat." She stood up.

"Do Miss Bertie and Miss Cornel'a have red hair like yours?"

"No, they have blonde hair like your mother does." Jillian didn't think this was the time to go into an explanation that her grandmother and great-aunt's hair color came out of a bottle these days.

Seemingly satisfied with that answer, Bonnie grabbed her mother's hand and Jillian's as they headed toward the restaurant. She skipped between them as they walked. "Do you like 'talian food, Miss Jillian? Mama and Daddy and I ate here before. I had fett'cine 'fredo. It was yummy." She looked at her mother. "Did I say that right?"

Lilith nodded. "Very close. It's *fettuccine Alfredo*."

Bonnie tried again. "Fett'cine *Al*-fredo. And they have ice cream here too, Miss Jillian, but they call it a funny name. What was that, Mama?"

"*Gelato.*"

"Gel-al-tol. Do you like gel-al-tol, Miss Jillian?"

"Yes I do."

"Did I say that right, Mama?"

"Not quite, but we'll work on it later."

"When we go to Wash'ton state together?"

"Wash*ing*ton state. Yes. After I come to pick you up from Belle Haven, we'll have a very long trip to make. We'll make a game of learning new words and learning to say them correctly while we're traveling."

Bonnie stopped skipping, bringing Lilith and Jillian to a stop also. She looked up at her mother. "I'm going to miss you, Mama, and Daddy too. You won't forget to come and get me, will you?"

Lilith leaned down and kissed her on the cheek. "That would be the last thing in the world I would ever forget. As soon as

Daddy and I have all our things moved into our new house, I will be on the next plane to come back to Georgia to get you. In the meantime, Miss Jillian will look after you."

She looked at Jillian and smiled. "That's okay then. I like her."

When Bonnie said that and looked at her with such an open expression of warmth, Jillian felt a little tug at her heart that she wasn't quite sure how to identify.

The restaurant door was just a few steps away, and Bonnie was about to speak again, but before she could Lilith took both of Bonnie's hands in hers and knelt down. "Now, before we go in, I want you to remember what I told you. You are to be very polite, and only speak when spoken to. It's fine to talk, but it's important to listen too."

"Yes, Mama."

Bonnie's expression was compliant, but Jillian wondered how difficult it would be for this precocious child to only listen. Would Bonnie listen to her if she had to discipline her? She began to feel a mild sense of panic. *What have I gotten myself into? I don't know anything about children. Heaven help me!*

I t was late afternoon before they returned to Belle Haven. Bonnie had shed a few tears when she said goodbye to her mother, but once she was strapped into her car seat and they were on the road, she cheered up, talking and asking questions which Cornelia mostly fielded, being in the back seat with the little girl. She told them about her friends and teacher at preschool, what she learned at Sunday school last week, about her favorite toys, and everything about the occasion of her fifth birthday when her mother and father took her to see *Snow White* at the Atlanta Ballet.

It wasn't until Jillian turned the car into the driveway at Belle Haven that there was a pause in Bonnie's conversation as she gazed at the impressive mansion. Jillian decided to take the loop to park in front of the house so that Bonnie could walk up the wide steps, past the white columns, and in through the front door with its cut-glass arched transom and side windows.

After Jillian had helped Bonnie out of the car, Bonnie grabbed her hand tightly. "Is this Belle Haven?" she asked.

"Yes it is. This will be your home for the next week or so."

Bonnie looked it over from side to side, from bottom to top and took a deep breath of satisfaction. "It's just like a palace. Does it make you feel like a princess to live here?"

"Well, not exactly."

"Why not?"

Bertie and Cornelia had already begun walking up the steps to the house. Before Jillian could think of a suitable answer, Cornelia stopped and turned to say, "I'm going up to my room, dears. I think we'll do something simple for supper this evening—soup and sandwiches maybe." She then continued on her way.

Bertie had unlocked the door and held it open for Cornelia. "I'm going to my room as well. I'll see you at suppertime." She followed her sister inside.

Looks like it will just be Bonnie and me the rest of the afternoon.

"Let's get your things from the trunk and carry them inside. Then I'll give you a tour of the house so you'll be able to find your way around." She paused. "Unless you're tired and want to take a nap?"

"Oh no, Miss Jillian. I couldn't sleep now. I want to see everything!"

By the time supper was over, Jillian felt exhausted. She didn't think she'd ever answered so many questions in a single day in her entire life. Bonnie had been thrilled with the play area that Jillian had arranged in the living room, the table and chairs being the perfect size for her. Jillian only hoped it would be enough to keep the girl occupied during the next several days so that she could get some work done.

While Bertie read a mystery novel and Cornelia crocheted a doily, Jillian and Bonnie unpacked the books from the crate and laid them across the coffee table so that Bonnie could look at them. Jillian set *Mrs. Beeton's Book of Household Management* and the yellow flour-mill booklet to one side.

"Which one would you like me to read to you before bedtime?" asked Jillian.

Bonnie ran her hand along the covers. She picked up one and looked at it for a moment. "What is this one called?"

"*A Little Princess*. It was one of my favorite stories when I was a little girl."

"Did you live here when you were little like me?"

"I came here a lot, but I lived with my parents in a house not far from here."

"Why don't you live with them now?"

"Well, my parents sold their house a long time ago and bought a motor home so they could travel. They don't live around here anymore."

"Do you miss them?"

The question caught Jillian by surprise. "Yes, I do miss them sometimes." She glanced up to see if Bertie and Cornelia were listening. Neither appeared to be distracted from her activity. "Now then, would you like me to read *A Little Princess* to you? We can do a couple chapters each night."

"Okay. If you like it, it must be good."

Later, after Bonnie had brushed her teeth, washed her face, and put on a white floral cotton nightgown, Jillian tucked Bonnie in the cot she'd set up in her own bedroom, together with the little gray stuffed bunny Bonnie had brought along, whom she called "Mr. Benj'min." Jillian had turned to get a chair so she could sit down next to the cot to read, but before she could step away, Bonnie threw back the covers and jumped out of bed.

"Miss Jillian, we almost forgot to pray!" The little girl got down on her knees next to the cot and bowed her head over clasped hands.

"Now I lay me down to sleep,
I pray the Lord my soul to keep.
If I should die before I wake,
I pray the Lord my soul to take.

"God bless Mama and Daddy, Grandma and Grandpa Trueblood, Grandma and Grandpa Winston, Grandmamma Gen'vieve, and Miss Jillian, Miss Bertie, and Miss Cornel'a. Amen."

She hopped back into the cot, pulled up the covers, and cradled Mr. Benjamin in the crook of one arm. "I'm ready now."

Jillian got the chair, sat down, and started reading, "'Chapter one. Once on a dark winter's day, . . .'" By the time she had read to the end of the second chapter, Bonnie had nearly given up her struggle to keep her eyes open. Jillian closed the book and just sat silently for a moment until the little girl's eyes closed completely and she was sure Bonnie was sound asleep.

She quietly laid the book on her nightstand and then returned the chair to its place. She had planned to go up to the third floor to look for a doll or two, the quilted pads for the little chairs, plus a few other things, but even though it was early, she felt so tired she decided to get ready for bed herself. By the time she came out of the bathroom, the lights over the circular staircase had been turned off, an indication that Bertie and Cornelia were also making an early night of it.

Jillian was in bed and felt like she had just fallen asleep when she heard a loud clap of thunder followed closely by a high-pitched scream. She tumbled out of bed and looked at the red numbers on the clock to see it was 2:23 in the morning. She felt confused and wondered where all the noise was coming from. Lightning flashed outside the window, making the room look like midday for a moment. Jillian caught sight of the cot where Bonnie was, reminding her that the little girl was in the room with her. The thunder crashed again, even louder, and Bonnie screamed again. Heavy drops of rain began to pelt the window with force. Jillian ran to Bonnie and took her in her arms, holding her close and telling her everything was all right.

There was a knock on the door. "Are you two okay?" asked Cornelia.

Bonnie's arms were locked tightly around Jillian's neck. She placed her hand over Bonnie's ear and called, "We're okay, Aunt Cornelia. Just a little scared by the thunder. You can go back to bed."

Jillian heard a muffled reply and then nothing else from her aunt. She carried Bonnie over to her bed and sat on the edge with the little girl on her lap. Her shoulder was wet with Bonnie's tears. She reached to her nightstand to turn on the lamp and then grabbed a tissue.

As she wiped the little girl's cheeks and then her nose, she cooed, "It's all right, Bonnie. It's just a storm. You're safe here with me. And Belle Haven has withstood lots of storms, even worse ones than this."

Bonnie sniffled. "May I sleep with you tonight?"

Jillian didn't even have to think about it. "Of course you may."

It was an arrangement that continued for the rest of Bonnie's stay at Belle Haven.

"That was a real Georgia gully washer last night," said Cornelia at breakfast. "It's supposed to be clear today, but I walked out to the barn this morning, and it's a muddy mess out there, with standing puddles everywhere. We won't be able to do any planting today. I already called Virgil and asked if he and Stan could come tomorrow instead." Virgil and Stan were cousins of Lenora's who had been of considerable help in the garden, despite occasional blowups between Virgil and Cornelia.

"Will that be enough time?" asked Jillian. "I promised Mrs.

Smith we'd have the landscaping around the barn finished before filming."

"I might ask a couple of ladies from the garden club to give us a hand too. I'll call Gladys and Lucille to see if they're available."

"What about your so-called 'investigator' friends and their ghost gadgets?" asked Bertie. "I thought they were coming over tomorrow."

Cornelia looked decidedly peeved. "They called to cancel yesterday afternoon. We'll have to put it off until next week since Mrs. Smith and her crew are going to be here Wednesday morning."

"Well, at least that's one silver lining," said Bertie, standing up. "I've got to get going. Lenora will be wondering what's keeping me."

After Bertie left, Jillian, still in her nightgown and bathrobe, stood up too. "I'm going to get showered and changed before Bonnie wakes up. You can leave the dishes, Aunt Cornelia. I'll tidy up after Bonnie has breakfast. Mrs. Fleming should be here about nine to get the regular cleaning done, and she'll come again tomorrow to get the extra bedrooms ready for our guests."

When Cornelia didn't answer, Jillian looked more closely at her aunt's expression. Worry lines furrowed her forehead. "What is it? You know, I can help with the planting too. I'm sure we can give Bonnie a little spade or something to keep her occupied."

"It's not the planting I'm worried about. I'd hoped that my friends from the LPI could come before the TV crew arrives."

"LPI?"

"Lowlands Paranormal Investigators. You remember. You went to one of their meetings with me a while back."

"How could I forget?" Jillian was beginning to feel like another cup of coffee was called for.

Cornelia looked at her with piercing blue eyes. "Careful, dear. You're starting to sound like your grandmother. Of course Bertie pooh-poohs it like she always does, and I know you agree with her, but something unnatural is going on."

"Like what?"

"Strange noises, things moved or missing. I've found the door wide open when I knew I closed it. I left my keys one place and they turned up in another. Last Thursday, when Mr. Hepplewhite was installing one of the chandeliers, he found a wrench that had been missing lying on one of the beams."

"Couldn't he have left it there last time?"

"It wasn't his. It was the plumber's, and he was never up a ladder. It must be a spirit we've disturbed. I can feel it."

Jillian was about to say that there must be a logical explanation, though she knew that comment would fall on deaf ears, when she had an idea. "What if we ask Pastor Keith to come over today or tomorrow, if he has time, and give the place a blessing?" She quickly added, "There's no need to tell him you think there's a poltergeist, we'll just ask him to say a few words. We'll christen it Belle Haven Hall."

Cornelia brightened a bit. "That could work. Bringing positive energy like that into the space could calm the spirits."

"I'll call him later this morning."

Cornelia stood and gave her great-niece a hug. "You're a good girl. I don't know how Bertie and I got along without you before you came back to Moss Hollow."

Early on Wednesday morning, the set-up crew arrived with a huge truck full of equipment for the television show. Upon conquering the overgrown jungle portion of Belle Haven's acreage, Cornelia and her band had discovered the remains of the original dirt track that led to the barn from the road and laid a last-minute load of gravel over it. It was just enough to make the path usable for the workmen who came and went, but it was not engineered sufficiently for the heavy truck to pull up to the building, especially with the recent rain, so the truck was parked at the side of the road that ran in front of Belle Haven.

Using handcarts, the crew unloaded large boxes from the back of the trailer, loaded them into a van, and then drove the van to the former tobacco barn, unloading the boxes to cart them into the building. This process was repeated multiple times.

While Bonnie was having breakfast under the watchful eye of Cornelia back at the house, Jillian stood inside the barn—now officially christened Belle Haven Hall, courtesy of Pastor Keith—watching the activity and answering questions. The pastor had come over the previous day at midmorning, assuring Jillian that he had often been asked to pronounce a blessing over a home or new business, and that it was no problem. Cornelia was obviously pleased, and even Bertie couldn't find a reason to be against the pastor's blessing, though she couldn't be present since she had to be at the bakery. Bonnie was quiet when the pastor spoke, apparently having been instructed on how to behave in church.

In fact, afterward, she asked Jillian if the barn was a church now, and had half a dozen follow-up questions when Jillian explained that it was not.

A voice with a strong New England accent interrupted Jillian's thoughts. "This will be our sixth episode to film, so we have the set-up routine down to a science now, but even so, the individual venues require that we do some tweaking."

Mrs. Smith—Patricia, as she had asked to be called—had walked over to stand next to Jillian. Fastidious in her appearance, the shrewd businesswoman wore a sharp navy-blue jacket and skirt, white blouse, and navy flats. Her chin-length gray hair was perfectly coifed, and she wore simple gold earrings and a light-gray scarf at her neck. She made Jillian feel rather underdressed in her short-sleeved black shirt, khaki pants, and tennis shoes, in spite of the labor-intensive atmosphere. Jillian made a mental note to take more pains with her appearance tomorrow when the rest of the guests were to arrive.

Patricia and the show's director had arrived at Belle Haven that morning about the same time as the truck. Houston Grier—a portly man in his late fifties with an unkempt beard and a brown fedora that had seen better days—was in the middle of the activity, instructing the men where he wanted the workstations set up so the cameraman could easily move between them to film the bakers as they worked.

Each of the five workstations consisted of a long counter with a built-in cooktop, a small oven, and a refrigerator/freezer. All the baking paraphernalia needed for the contestant to meet his or her challenge—pots, pans, spoons, spatulas, you name it—were placed on shelves below the counter.

"Would you care to come up to the house, or are you needed here?" Jillian asked Patricia.

"The crew can handle it with Houston here to keep an eye on

things. I do want to talk to you about tomorrow afternoon when the contestants and the judges arrive, and it would be quieter away from here."

After they left the hall, as they started up the garden path toward the house, Patricia began to explain that she wanted a tea to be prepared for Thursday afternoon at Belle Haven, so that all the principals could discuss the expectations and schedule for the coming days.

"That is easily done," said Jillian. "I'll ask my grandmother to deliver a variety of baked goods from The Chocolate Shoppe."

"You seem to have a good business going there. I look forward to trying out some of its wares. I'll leave the particulars of the tea up to you, but I think that we'll gather at four o'clock. Do you have a room that will accommodate us? There will be nine altogether."

"If it's agreeable, you could use the living room. There is plenty of seating there. Or, if you prefer, it could be set up in the dining room."

"I'll have a look when we get there and then decide."

"Okay." Jillian scanned her memory trying to think of something to say to the successful older woman. "After you were here last time, I looked at my grandmother's copy of *Blissful Baking* to check out the copyright date. It's from 1969."

"Then it's a first edition."

Jillian glanced at Patricia's profile as they walked. There was something almost sad in her expression. It struck Jillian as strange, considering how successful the cookbook had been.

"How many times has it been reprinted?" asked Jillian.

"We've updated it every ten years, changing the photographs, tweaking the measurements in some cases."

"Really? Since I've been learning the bakery business, I've made several of the recipes from that cookbook, trying to improve my baking skills. I have to say that everything I've tried of yours has come out pretty much perfect, and that's saying something about the recipes, since the baker was a beginner at best."

"Well, times change. People want to see less salt, other options for fats, and so forth. It's coming up on the fiftieth anniversary very soon, and we're already working on a new edition for that, adding some gluten-free recipes."

Jillian chuckled. "Gluten-free is something we don't do at The Chocolate Shoppe. I can just imagine if I suggested it to Bertie. She'd have a cow."

"I understand her point of view, but it's something lots of people are interested in. It's not that easy to find really good gluten-free baked goods, but it can be done. You might consider looking into it. There's definitely a market for it right now among those who have allergies and those who believe it's a healthier lifestyle."

"Until the next new thing."

Patricia smiled. "Yes, until then."

They had reached the door of the mansion that opened into the kitchen/dining area, and Jillian stepped in to hold the door for Patricia. Inside, Cornelia was at the sink, washing the skillet she had used for breakfast.

"Where's Bonnie?" asked Jillian.

Cornelia looked up. "Oh, she's playing in the living room." She reached for a towel to dry her hands.

"Patricia, this is my aunt, Cornelia Montgomery. Aunt Cornelia, Patricia Smith, author of *Blissful Baking* among many other cookbooks, TV host, and now TV producer."

"Pleased to meet you." The two women shook hands.

"Patricia," Jillian said, "let me show you through to the living room first."

They had just left the kitchen when the doorbell sounded.

Cornelia called, "I'll get it!"

Entering the living room, Jillian couldn't see Bonnie until

she walked closer to the sofa and looked over the back of it. She was sitting at the little table, carefully coloring a picture in one of the coloring books Jillian had purchased. When the little girl looked up and saw Jillian, she smiled, dropped her crayon, and ran around the sofa to hug Jillian's legs. "Oh, I missed you!"

"Now, Bonnie. I wasn't gone that long."

She looked up with her big blue eyes. "I still missed you." She turned her head to look at Patricia.

"Is this your daughter?" asked Patricia.

"Oh my goodness, no. This is Bonnie Trueblood, a cousin. She's staying here a few days. Bonnie, this is Mrs. Smith."

Bonnie did as she had when she met Jillian in the parking lot at the restaurant. She walked to Patricia and extended her hand. "I'm pleased to meet you, Mrs. Smith."

Patricia shook hands with the child. "Likewise." To Jillian she said, "What a lovely child," as if Bonnie couldn't hear her.

"I—"

Jillian was interrupted by a commotion in the hallway outside the door. She turned to see a young man wearing jeans and a green T-shirt backing through the door carrying something large covered by a cloth. On the other side, Jillian saw the face of Burton Puckett peeking around the edge.

"Clear that coffee table!" he ordered. Jillian automatically picked up the children's books she had left there since Sunday, stacking the yellow booklet and the *Mrs. Beeton's* on top, and placed them on the floor next to the wall near the end of the sofa. Then she hurriedly cleared the various magazines and a large, flat dish containing a hodgepodge of items.

Burton and the young man, whom Jillian now recognized as Burton's grandson, Gerald, came forward and, as gently as they could, placed the item on the table. Burton stood up straight and flexed his hands. "Pardon me for that rude entrance, but our burden was somewhat heavy."

"You always did like to make an entrance," said Cornelia, who had followed them in. The two had known each other since high school, though they hadn't always been as friendly as they currently were. "I would've come ahead to clear the table before you started to carry it in if you'd given me a chance."

"Well, I am sorry about that, Cornelia, but we have to do this quick. I'm supposed to get Gerald to the high school on time this morning since he's helping me out." Burton grinned. "And I can't deny that I enjoy a dramatic entrance." To Gerald he said, "Run out to the truck and get that package from the back seat."

"Yes, sir," Gerald said, even as he moved quickly out of the room. It was amusing to Jillian how Gerald seemed to be a somewhat shy young man of few words compared to his father and grandfather, both of whom never met a stranger.

While Gerald was out of the room, Jillian made the introductions. Gerald returned shortly, holding a large box wrapped in paper with a pretty pattern of pink roses.

Looking at Bonnie, Burton tilted his head toward the cloth-covered structure, which was obviously the old dollhouse. "Would you like to see what's underneath the sheet?"

"Yes please!"

Burton removed the cloth with a flourish. He had restored the dollhouse beyond Jillian's expectations. Not only was the exterior painted the same yellow as Belle Haven and the columns white, but when he fixed the roof, he had added a round opening filled with a golden-yellow translucent material embossed with star shapes and fleurs-de-lis to mimic Belle Haven's stained-glass dome. Each of the interior rooms had been papered with different light-colored vintage-looking wallpaper, and the floors were painted in coordinating colors to go with the wallpapers.

"Oh, Burton, this is lovely. You must let me pay you for all your hard work."

"Nonsense. It was my pleasure. This is the most fun I've had on a project in a long time," the older man said as his grandson came back into the room. "I used old wallpaper samples from the hardware store. And there's a little something more. Gerald, give that to this little lady."

Gerald carefully handed the package to Bonnie. She had to hold it with her arms as wide apart as possible. Her eyes were even wider than normal. "It's for me?"

Burton nodded.

She looked up at Jillian. "May I open it?"

"Of course. Let's put it on the sofa so you can manage it."

"My Doris saved everything, including old wrapping paper," Burton said while Bonnie carefully removed the feminine-looking paper. "I haven't had the heart to throw anything away since she passed, but I was glad I had something on hand I could wrap this in. She would've been pleased to know I actually used some of it."

Bonnie clapped her hands with delight when she removed the paper from the top of the box. It contained a variety of dollhouse furniture and beautiful handmade dolls. She ran her hand over the clear-plastic front and then looked up at Jillian for a moment before turning toward Burton and Gerald who were standing next to each other.

"Thank you! It's just like Christmas!"

"You're welcome, little lady," said Burton. "We've had that just gathering dust in the back room of the store since Christmastime— one of the things from our inventory that no one bought last season, and I knew it would be perfect for you to play with."

"Then you must let me pay for that at least, Burton," said Jillian.

"Absolutely not. This is my present for the sweet little girl. The look on her face is worth the price and more." He smiled at

Bonnie and then stole a quick look at Cornelia that was . . . Jillian wasn't quite sure what it was. According to Burton himself, he'd been sweet on Cornelia in high school. Could it be? *I wonder if he has a crush on Aunt Cornelia again after all these years.*

It felt as if Belle Haven was full to the rafters with people the following afternoon. The doorbell began ringing after lunch, and it seemed to Jillian as though she had been continuously getting people settled in their rooms ever since. She was certainly getting her exercise that day, walking up and down the circular stairs.

It was fortunate that Burton had delivered the dollhouse since it helped to keep Bonnie occupied most of the time. Before he and Gerald had left, they set the dollhouse on the floor, its front side facing the wall so that Bonnie could reach the rooms of the top level, since the structure was almost the same height as she was. She would periodically seek out Jillian to give her a hug and to ask several questions, but Jillian was getting used to this intrusion on her thoughts and time, discovering she had more patience than she had given herself credit for. It was easy to be patient with Bonnie.

Patricia had given Jillian a list of people she should expect, so when she opened the door and they introduced themselves, she already had some idea who they were. Besides their names, the list included their home city and state, what they did for a living, and their role in the show. Since Patricia was the producer and Houston was the director, the only things left were either judge or contestant.

The first arrival, Victor Varga, introduced himself as the host judge. He explained that he was in every episode to provide continuity. Jillian had actually seen him on television before, in an infomercial where he hawked special kitchen gadgets that he had invented. He was from Chicago and looked to be about thirty years old. He was dressed neatly, but he had the type of facial hair that is meant to look unkempt. His short black hair stood up all over, making it look as though he'd walked through a hedge backward. The overall impression was that of a porcupine.

The next person to arrive was the regional judge for the Deep South. She was Florence Oglethorpe, whom Jillian had also seen on TV in a cooking program out of Atlanta. Florence was what Jillian would call a "big blonde." It wasn't that she was all that large, but her hair was big, and her voice was as loud as her clothes—she showed up at the door in a matching top and capris made of fabric covered with large bright-red and purple flowers.

The first contestant to arrive was Waldon Radcliffe, identified as an antiquarian from Alabama on Patricia's list. He was a rather nondescript, soft-spoken, middle-aged man with mouse-brown hair and pale skin, as if he stepped outdoors only when absolutely necessary, who smelled faintly of pipe tobacco and wintergreen mints. He was delighted with the historical Belle Haven, particularly the impressive two-story library, and actually seemed pleased when Jillian showed him to his small room on the third floor. She hoped all the contestants would be as agreeable.

Avery Hadley, a florist from South Carolina, and Chester Dale, a retired dentist turned bookshop owner now living in Key West, showed up at the same time. It was a fortunate thing for Avery, as she had arrived with no less than five pieces of matching luggage in various sizes and two boxes, and Chester was gracious enough to help her inside with all of it, having only one large bag and a backpack himself.

Jillian guessed that Avery was late middle-aged. She tended slightly toward the plump side and her honey-blonde hair was swept into a neat cap. It was obvious that she had taken great care with her outfit, her accessories and shoes perfectly coordinated with her skirt and blouse. With so much luggage for just a few days' stay, Jillian thought she must be the type to change outfits during the day according to the occasion. She would not be surprised to see her in different outfits for the tea and at dinnertime.

Chester appeared to have taken to the island life, his long gray hair gathered into a ponytail at his neck and extending down to the middle of his back. She couldn't imagine her own dentist wearing his hair that way. Chester had the tanned skin of someone who was perpetually out in the sun and wore cutoffs, flip-flops, and a light cotton button-up open over a T-shirt that had "Key West" written above a sketched portrait of Ernest Hemingway.

Bonnie happened to be at Jillian's side when she opened the front door of Belle Haven for Dorothea Woods, an African-American elementary school teacher from Mississippi. She definitely had the demeanor of a teacher, engaging Bonnie in conversation so well that Bonnie accompanied them up the stairs and into what was to be Dorothea's bedroom during her stay. It was only when Jillian firmly said that she needed to let Dorothea have some time to get settled, promising that she could talk with her later, that Bonnie agreed to go back downstairs with Jillian.

Kaylee Sinclair was the last of the contestants to arrive and was Georgia's contribution to the mix. A recent college graduate in her early twenties who was listed as a nurse, she reminded Jillian of the cheerleaders she'd known in high school and college. The young woman was full of energy and optimism. She made Jillian wistful for her college days.

As soon as Kaylee was settled in one of the bedrooms, Jillian raced downstairs to the kitchen to get the tea started, as it was twenty minutes to four. She had hoped to have the tea ready to serve at four on the dot, but she wasn't sure she could manage it now.

She needn't have worried. Cornelia had already started heating the water for the tea and was arranging a variety of baked goods that Bertie had brought home with her on several doily-lined china plates.

"Where's Bertie?" asked Jillian.

"She was tuckered out when she got home, so she's gone to her room to get a nap."

"Thanks for getting a handle on this," said Jillian. "I hadn't thought about how much time it would take to just get people settled in their rooms." She grabbed a tray that held vintage teacups, plus the matching saucers and silver teaspoons. She was glad she had thought to bring all of them into the kitchen from the huge china cabinet in the dining room that morning.

Patricia, Houston, Waldon, and Dorothea had already gathered in the living room. Bonnie was having another one of her "deep" conversations with Dorothea. Jillian came in to hear the child ask, "Do you like teaching kind'garten?" Patricia and Houston were engaged in conversation with Waldon, but the antiquarian still occasionally glanced with undisguised annoyance at the child. Jillian could just imagine Bonnie asking him what an "ant'quar'an" was. *Time to nip this in the bud.*

She placed the tray on the coffee table that she had earlier covered with a pretty tea-dyed linen cloth edged with tatted lace. "Bonnie, would you come with me a moment?"

Bonnie smiled. "Yes, Miss Jillian!"

She walked Bonnie into the library and closed the door. She asked her to sit in a wooden desk chair and pulled up another one to sit across from her. She tried to think how to begin. Bonnie hadn't really done anything wrong, but as her mother had said, there were times when it was better to only speak when spoken to. Thinking of how Lilith had handled the situation, Jillian took Bonnie's hands in hers.

"Bonnie, you have been a very good girl. But while all these people are here, I need you to play with your toys and let the grown-ups talk among themselves. They're here for a very important purpose, and they need to concentrate on learning what they need to do."

"Is it like school?"

"In a way. Miss Patricia and Mr. Houston—"

"Is that the man with the fluffy beard and funny hat?"

"Yes, but please don't call it a 'funny' hat."

"Why not? Don't you think it's funny?"

"It's not polite to say so. As I was saying . . ." She paused. *What was I saying?* "Bonnie, I just need you to play with your toys quietly while the grown-ups are talking and having tea. In fact, would you like to have your own tea with some treats from Miss Bertie's bakery?"

"Yes, please. Would you have tea with me?"

"I can't right now, sweetheart, but I will set it up at the little table and you can pretend to have tea with the dolls and Mr. Benjamin. And if you are good and quiet, I promise that in a few days, after all these people have left, you and I will have a special tea, just the two of us."

"Okay. I will be extra good."

Jillian leaned forward and kissed Bonnie's forehead. "That's perfect then. You run along and play."

By the time Jillian brought in the last tray that held two large teapots full of steaming tea, all the visitors were gathered in the living room. As she was about to go fetch the child's-size tea that she had prepared for Bonnie, Avery, who had indeed changed from her traveling outfit into a dress that was, appropriately, tea length, exclaimed, "Oh, you have a *Mrs. Beeton's!*"

Avery reached over from her spot at the end of the sofa to pick up the top book from the stack Jillian had placed on the floor when the dollhouse was delivered. Avery held the book like it was the Holy Grail and gazed around the room. The other occupants of the room looked at her with puzzled expressions. "I'm afraid I'm a bit of an Anglophile. I just love all things British. You all know about *Mrs. Beeton's Book of Household Management*, don't you? It's sold millions of copies in the UK since it was first published during the reign of Queen Victoria." When no one answered, she opened the book to the copyright page. "From 1927. That's not terribly early, but a respectable date. I have a copy from 1895 myself, though there are much earlier editions if you can find them. I also have the newest edition, of course." She put the book on her lap. "And what's this?" She picked up the yellow booklet and gave it a cursory glance before placing it on the coffee table. She picked up the next book. "Oh, it's an old copy of *Peter Rabbit*." She flipped the pages. "How charming. Beatrix Potter was quite a woman. My husband and I visited her farm, Hill Top, in Cumbria County, when we took a guided tour of England last year. Of course it's in the hands of the National Trust now, and the house is a museum, so it's just as she kept it. It's absolutely charming."

"May I see that?" asked Dorothea. "Children still love her stories. I often read them to my kindergartners."

Avery passed it to her and continued to pick up the books, one at a time, making a comment on each one, and then passing them along to Dorothea, who in turn passed each one along to others in the room, some of whom seemed interested, some not. Avery kept the *Mrs. Beeton's* in her lap until Kaylee asked to see it.

Jillian left the room to get Bonnie's tea, and when she returned, the focus of the adults was on their own tea. Avery was expertly pouring each cupful. The books had been stacked on the small side table next to the chair where Bertie usually sat, and where Chester, the long-haired dentist, was currently sitting. Jillian walked over and picked up the stack of books, intending to take them into the library.

"Oh, Jillian," said Avery. "Would you mind terribly if I were to take your *Mrs. Beeton's* to my room later to peruse? I'd love to see how it differs from my copies."

"Of course. I'm just going to set these in the library. Help yourself."

When she returned, she sat at the periphery of the group, planning to take notes herself on the information that Patricia was going to give, but it wasn't necessary as Victor handed around an itinerary. Jillian wondered if Patricia had an assistant, and if she did, why that person wasn't with her. *Just as well*, she thought, *I'd have to give up my bedroom if there was another person, and Bonnie and I would end up sleeping in the attic.*

Friday was sunny and hot—another typical late-summer Georgia day. Jillian would have liked nothing better than to enjoy a lazy day, but with a houseful of guests, that was out of the question. It was to be the first day of filming, and while the contestants and judges finished their breakfasts, Jillian and Bonnie accompanied Patricia to check out how things were going with the crew in the barn. Houston was already there—she could hear him bellowing out orders as they neared the building. Jillian had given him an extra key earlier that morning so he could open the barn for the crew.

"Looks like you might have some pranksters around these parts," said Houston when they entered the hall. "Or a ghost." He smirked when he said the last three words.

"What do you mean?" asked Jillian.

"The door was open when I got here, and some of the cooking utensils had been messed with, scattered on the floor. No real damage done, just an annoyance for the crew to check and get everything washed and back in place. Fortunately, the ingredients hadn't been delivered yet."

"I'm so sorry," said Jillian. "I don't understand how that could have happened." She thought of what Aunt Cornelia had said about strange occurrences. Could a ghost move things? She shook her head. *Now she's got me doing it.* "I'll call the police to check it out. Maybe they can put out an extra patrol."

"That might not be a bad idea," said Patricia, "but we can't afford to put off the first day's shoot. Ask them to come after we're finished for the day." She looked up and around at the four corners of the large room. "Do you have any security cameras?"

"No, I'm afraid not."

"Well, we have a lot of expensive equipment here. If someone can break in that easily, you may have to hire a night watchman while we're here to see that nothing is disturbed."

Jillian sighed inwardly. *Where am I going to find a night watchman? How much is that going to cost?* "I'll take care of it."

She would have liked to stick around to see how the filming went, but she was needed back at the house to help clean up after breakfast and to start preparing a lunch buffet for the cast and crew. Fortunately, the crew was on their own for evening meals, so she only had to worry about feeding nine extra people that night. *Only nine.* It sounded like a lot, but she had to admit the supper on the previous evening had gone well, and it was only for three more evenings.

On the way back to the house, she and Bonnie passed the judges and contestants en route to the hall. Their spirits seemed high, and they chatted with each other amicably. All of the contestants carried matching tote bags with *The All-American Baking Contest* emblazoned across the sides.

When she opened the kitchen door for Bonnie, she saw two familiar women standing at the kitchen island cutting up broccoli and celery for a veggie tray already heaped with bell peppers, cauliflower, and baby carrots. It was Maudie Honeycutt and Wanda Jean Maplewood, fellow Sweetie Pies. They always volunteered to help out in a pinch, but the thing was, they had a penchant for gossip, and even worse, a tendency to get it completely wrong.

Cornelia was rinsing dishes at the sink to put in the dishwasher. "I mean, honestly, what sort of gentleman doesn't remove his hat indoors?" Jillian knew she meant Houston, having heard the comment previously when Cornelia and Bertie discussed it. They had not yet seen him without his tatty brown fedora.

"No gentleman at all, if you ask me," replied Wanda Jean. "Although, I suppose he might be bald. Some men prefer to cover that up."

"Or maybe it's a 'thing'—like a signature trademark," said Maudie. "Celebrities do that, you know. Like that singer who always wears orange."

"What singer is that?" asked Wanda Jean.

"I don't know. I can't remember his name." She paused. "It might have been purple."

"His name is Purple?"

"No, it might have been that he wore purple clothes."

"I think you're just making that up."

Maudie appeared to be mildly outraged. "I am not. I—"

"Good morning, ladies," Jillian interrupted strategically. "How nice of you to come to help us out." She thought it was better to interrupt than to let Maudie and Wanda Jean get wound up. Sometimes it was amazing to her how the two women managed to remain such close friends. She distracted them further by introducing them to Bonnie, and as expected, they cooed and fussed over her. Bonnie in turn was happy to have their attention and oblige their questions, firing back with questions of her own.

Jillian considered telling Cornelia that someone had been in the hall overnight, but stopped herself just in time. Besides feeding Cornelia's assumption that ghosts haunted the old structure, she could just imagine the gossip that would rage around Moss Hollow once Maudie and Wanda Jean got hold of it. She decided to play it safe and not mention it.

"I need to make a quick phone call. Is it okay if Bonnie stays in here with you all for a few minutes?"

"Of course she can," said Maudie.

Bonnie didn't hesitate to climb up on a stool next to the counter where Maudie and Wanda Jean were working. Sitting with her legs folded beneath her and her forearms on the counter, she had a bird's-eye view of the activity. "May I cut up some veg'ables too?"

Jillian was already headed out of the kitchen toward her little office near the front of the house where she could have some privacy, but she almost stopped to answer Bonnie's question. "Absolutely not" was on the tip of her tongue, but she decided that if three women, two of whom were well past the age of seventy, couldn't deal with one five-year-old child, she didn't know who could.

In her office, she sat down and took out her cell phone to call the sheriff's office. She felt a great reluctance to make the call. This wasn't an emergency situation, so she wasn't going to call 911—this time. How many other people in Moss Hollow had the ten-digit number for the local police in their speed dial? She wasn't quite sure how she had become "that person"—the one who always seemed to be present when something suspicious happened. She thought of her first week back in Moss Hollow after a twenty-year absence, and how she had been suspected of a crime she didn't commit. Ever since, it seemed that Deputy Goodman Jones was often on hand to insinuate she'd done something wrong.

She shook her head and thought of his nickname since high school, "Gooder." The deputy's grandmother had once voiced suspicions that Jillian had designs on her grandson. The idea that she felt that sort of attraction toward Gooder was ludicrous, and thankfully the embarrassing confrontation had happened long enough ago that Jillian could laugh about it now. She took a deep breath and tapped the screen, hoping and praying she'd be able to talk to Laura Lee Zane, another deputy at the police department. The difference was that Laura Lee was a dear friend and fellow Sweetie Pie who didn't constantly suspect Jillian of whatever crime she was reporting.

"Deputy Jones," said the familiar voice on the line.

Good grief. If this is any indication of my luck today, I

should've stayed in bed. She cleared her throat. "Hello, Gooder. It's Jillian."

She could almost hear his sneer. "Hey, Jillian. What's up? Find a body in your bathtub this morning?"

"No, but thanks for asking." She didn't even try to keep the tone of sarcasm out of her voice. "I'm calling because there was a break-in at Belle Haven Hall last night."

He sounded confused. "The mansion was broken into?"

"No. Belle Haven Hall is the name we've given the old tobacco barn we're converting."

"Well, isn't that hoity-toity. What was stolen?"

"Well, nothing was taken that I know of, but the door was wide open and some things had been moved around."

"Was anything damaged?"

Jillian couldn't help but sigh. "Not that I know of."

"I guess I could come over and brush for prints."

Jillian wished she'd thought this through a bit better. "The thing is, we've got a TV crew here and they're going to be filming in the barn—I mean, the hall, today. In fact, I'm sure that everything that was disturbed has been washed and replaced, and I suppose with all the people going in and out, any footprints outside or fingerprints on the door are probably smudged away."

"Then why did you call?" he asked, irritation plain.

I wish I hadn't, she thought, but then remembered what she'd told Patricia. "I was hoping y'all could increase the patrols by Belle Haven, at least while the TV crew is here."

"Do you think we are at your personal beck and call? We don't have the extra manpower to devote to just driving by your place all the time."

"Okay. Then could you recommend someone I could hire as a night watchman?"

"How much are you paying?" he asked.

"I guess whatever the going rate is for night watchmen." She was quick to add, "But not, you know, an exorbitant amount."

There was a pause, then Gooder asked, "What time would you need this guy?"

"I guess from about ten or eleven at night until about six in the morning."

"How many nights?"

"Just while the film crew is here. They're leaving Monday, so three nights, I guess."

"All right. There will be someone there at ten this evening."

"Who is this person?"

There was no answer. "Gooder? Are you there?" She looked at the screen. Gooder had hung up. *Great. Who knows what sort of loser he'll send over?* She thought about calling him back to tell him to forget it, that she would find her own night watchman, but she knew she didn't have the time or even know where to start. She'd have to wait until ten o'clock that evening to find out to whom she would be entrusting the safety of her clients' expensive equipment.

The table in Belle Haven's dining room extended to seat twelve people, so there was plenty of room for the nine guests at the mansion to have dinner in the evenings. Jillian, Bertie, Cornelia, and Bonnie would have their evening meal at six in the breakfast nook right off the kitchen as usual, before all their guests came down for dinner at seven. That way, they were free to serve their guests' meal, and Bonnie was fed and could play a while in the living room before Jillian trundled up to bed with her at eight.

That plan had worked well the previous evening, so Jillian saw no reason to change anything.

However, when the contestants came back to the house in the late afternoon Jillian could feel the tension in the air. Whatever friendliness they had shown to one another that morning seemed to have evaporated for the most part. Dorothea complained of a headache and asked if she might have dinner in her room. Chester and Kaylee disappeared to their rooms as well. Only Avery and Waldon seemed to be getting along. They settled in the living room and talked easily between themselves, mostly about all things British as both had taken tours of England.

The judges, Victor and Florence, arrived at the house shortly after the contestants. They obviously were not thrilled to be working together. Victor conveyed this with stony silence and piercing glances at his co-judge, and Florence with loud comments about how much she hated infomercials seeing as how "those people just hawk useless stuff to the unsuspecting public."

Understandably, Patricia was on edge as well. Saying she

needed to make some phone calls, she slipped into the library and closed the doors. Houston had yet to return.

Later, after Jillian had finished with her supper, she left Bonnie at the table with Bertie and Cornelia while she took a tray up to Dorothea. She knocked lightly on the door.

She heard the creak of the old box springs on the other side of the door, and after a few moments, Dorothea opened the door and peered around the edge. Seeing it was Jillian, she opened it wider and let her bring in the tray.

"How are you feeling?" asked Jillian.

"A bit better. I took a pain reliever and it seems to have done the trick." She looked at the tray. "I appreciate your bringing my meal up here though. I'm sorry to be a bother, but *those people*." She shook her head. "I don't think I could take another minute with them today."

"What happened out there?" She placed the tray on the bench at the end of the bed.

"I'm not entirely sure. At first, everyone seemed friendly enough, but this experience is not turning out to be what I thought it would be. I think it began this morning after we started filming when it became obvious to everyone that Florence is a handful. Victor is supposed to be the host but she was just loud and rude on and off camera, trying to upstage him and making jokes at his expense. And she was condescending to the competitors. The comments she made about our desserts were not just critical or even a little bit constructive—they were downright mean. She is not a nice woman."

Jillian could just imagine how all that went over with Patricia. "Maybe they can edit around her."

"I don't see how, but I hope you're right. The other thing is that I thought there would be camaraderie between the bakers, you know, that we'd be helping each other out, but when we started the actual competition something changed. When the camera was on, it was all smiles and compliments, but in between, people were snippy. Maybe it was just Florence's influence that changed everything. All I know for sure is that there is at least one among us who is bound and determined to win at any cost. I don't know who it was, but someone switched some labels on the spices I brought with me. It was only a stroke of luck that I caught it before the damage was done. It was almost a disaster."

"But that means someone would have gotten into your room here, doesn't it?"

"Yes. Which is why I'll be locking my door from here on out. You see, we were all told the types of things we would be baking on the show beforehand so we could bring our own recipes. Today was two different chocolate desserts, tomorrow it's a trifle in the morning and a decorated cake in the afternoon, and for Sunday afternoon it's a sweet or savory bread. We had to let them know all the ingredients that we require, but we're also allowed to bring any special ingredients we wanted ourselves—spices, herbs, liquors, what have you—and any particular pans or dishes we needed. I know that someone must have gotten into my room last night to change the labels since they were never out of my sight after I left the house this morning."

"Did something like that happen to anyone else?"

"I don't know. No one said anything. But then, neither did I. It seemed like there was enough going on with Houston trying to get Florence to be less unpleasant. I didn't want to cause even more trouble, especially when I had no idea who'd done it."

Dorothea looked a moment at her hands, which were shaking slightly, and then rubbed her temples with the tips of her fingers.

Jillian patted her shoulder. "Maybe you should just have your dinner and then relax up here. I'll come back for the tray later. And if it's all right with you, I'll talk to Patricia. I think she needs to know if someone is trying to cheat."

Dorothea agreed, and Jillian left and headed toward the stairs, where Chester joined her, rattling a set of keys in his hand. They started down the stairs side by side. "Say, I was thinking I'll just go out this evening and see what's happening in Moss Hollow. Is there a place, a pub maybe, where I can get a sandwich and a beer?"

"I'm afraid you may be disappointed about Moss Hollow's nightlife, even on a Friday evening. I've heard that Cap's Place makes good sandwiches, and they do serve beer, but I've never been in there myself. Still, you're welcome to stay and eat here. I guarantee it's a good meal."

They had reached the bottom of the steps, and Chester looked around with wide eyes when he heard Florence's loud chortle drifting toward them from the living room. "No offense. I'm sure it will be as wonderful a meal as last evening's was, but I just need to get away for a bit. Please offer my apologies to the others. I won't be out too late."

Jillian gave him the directions to Cap's, explaining that she thought it had more of a gentle, pub-like atmosphere as opposed to the bar scene he might be used to in Key West. He didn't seem to mind, and he strode to the front door and left.

Well, that's two less for dinner. She was about to go to the dining room to remove two of the place settings when Kaylee came hopping down the steps. She had a packet in her hand.

"Jillian, I was just coming to look for you. I was thinking of just having one of my meal-replacement shakes this evening." She shook the packet. "Could I borrow your blender and some milk?"

Jillian looked at the young woman's trim figure. Seemed like the last thing she needed was a meal replacement. "Well, sure. But we have plenty of vegetables and fruit and lean meat for dinner if you're watching your figure."

"Oh, it's not that so much. I'm just not all that hungry." She shook the packet again. "This little thing has all the vitamins and such that I need, so I'd just as soon have it."

Jillian looked closely at Kaylee's face, looking for signs of dissatisfaction as she'd seen on Dorothea's and Chester's. She tried to choose her words carefully. "Did anything . . . odd happen today?"

"You mean besides Florence making a fool of herself and being an absolute pill, Dorothea shaking like a leaf every time the camera was on her, Waldon putting on a stupid—not to mention terrible—British accent whenever they talked to him on camera, and Chester's 'secret ingredient' turning out to be illegal in this state? I don't know how they're going to work around that."

"What about Avery? Did she have any problems?"

"Oh no. Avery was aces. I'd say she was the winner today. They said my chocolate dessert was good, but it didn't have enough 'wow factor.' I'm going to have to up my game tomorrow."

"But there was nothing wrong with your ingredients or anything like that?"

"I don't think so. Why do you ask?"

"Oh, it's nothing. Just wondering."

Before Kaylee could inquire further, Jillian led her to the kitchen and showed her where the things she needed were. Possum was in the kitchen, lying under the table. Jillian hadn't seen much of him since the arrival of the guests yesterday, but he seemed to form a fast attachment to Kaylee, getting up from his relaxed place to wind his body around her legs. The feeling was mutual as Kaylee knelt down to rub his back and speak a few fawning words before standing to wash up and fix her shake.

Bertie and Cornelia had finished their meals and sent Bonnie to play in the living room, so they were getting the last-minute things ready for the guests' dinner. After Jillian told them that there would only be six for dinner, she went to the dining room to remove three of the place settings.

Their guests' meal was ready and on the table at seven as requested. Waldon and Avery sat on one side of the table, and Patricia and Victor were on the other side as Florence had already taken one of the end chairs. Houston hadn't shown up, but Patricia didn't seem worried, so Jillian thought he must be all right.

Jillian kept her eye on the food and drink to make sure everyone had what they needed. Listening to the conversation, she almost felt sorry for Florence—almost, but not quite, as she had brought this state of affairs upon herself by all accounts. The rest of the group engaged with each other and all but ignored her except for a few pointed comments when she tried to join in. She eventually lapsed into an obviously angry silence. After she'd eaten the dessert that had been served, she threw her napkin on the table, and said, "Well, I'm going to my room!" as if she'd just told them all off. The atmosphere lightened considerably once she'd departed.

By the time the remaining guests had left the dining room, it was Bonnie's bedtime. While Bertie and Cornelia cleared the table, Jillian took Bonnie up to her room to read a couple more chapters of *A Little Princess*. Bonnie no longer fell asleep during the story as she had the first night she was at Belle Haven. Jillian sat next to her on the bed where she was tucked in with her stuffed rabbit, and she listened with wide eyes, asking questions about words she didn't understand and shedding a few tears when sad things happened to the "little princess," Sara Crewe.

Jillian had forgotten that the Shirley Temple movie differed in many aspects from the book. "Bonnie, do you want to read a different book? Maybe a happier one?" she suggested.

Bonnie shook her head vehemently. "No, I want to know what happens to Sara."

Remembering that the story did eventually have a happy ending, Jillian acquiesced.

She read the last paragraph of the chapter they were on, then closed the book and told Bonnie, "I have to go downstairs and help clean up." She leaned over and kissed her on the forehead. "You go to sleep now, and I'll be back up soon."

"Will you leave the light on?"

"Of course. But you must promise to go to sleep." Jillian tried to sound stern, but had found that it really wasn't necessary with Bonnie.

"I promise." She put her hand on Jillian's arm and looked up with her big blue eyes. "Do you love me, Miss Jillian?"

Jillian felt her eyes well up. She had been surprised by how quickly she had formed an attachment to the little girl and how strong her feelings were. She put her hand over Bonnie's. "Yes I do."

"I love you too." She snuggled up with Mr. Benjamin and closed her eyes.

By the time the kitchen was cleaned and preparations that could be made for breakfast the next day had been completed, Jillian was exhausted. Cornelia and Bertie had already headed for bed, and the guests had gone to their rooms, except for Chester, who was still out, and Houston, who hadn't shown up at all. Jillian was ready to call it a night too, but it was nearly ten o'clock, and she had to walk out to the hall to meet the night watchman that Gooder had said he would send over. She was not looking forward to it.

It was dark, so she grabbed a flashlight and started down the path toward the hall. After all her activity, the coolness of the night air felt rather good. She had just unlocked the door when a police car pulled up to the building. Gooder, wearing a light jacket over a T-shirt and jeans, with a holster strapped to his belt, got out of the car and walked over to where Jillian was standing.

She was speechless for a moment, but was finally able to get a few words out. "What are you doing here?"

"I believe it's called 'moonlighting.'"

"*You're* the night watchman?"

"That's right."

Jillian still couldn't quite grasp it. "Why?"

"Not your concern. I'm getting paid for this, right? We need to talk terms."

Gooder followed Jillian into the hall, where all the lights had been left on. There was no sign of anyone. *Houston must have gone out to eat with the crew*, thought Jillian. *He could have at least let us know.* While she showed Gooder around the building, she told him about the odd things that had happened there, tactfully leaving out Cornelia's conclusions, and they came to an agreement about how much he would be paid.

She left Gooder, still flummoxed as to why he would have any need to moonlight. She knew he worked full-time for the county sheriff. She wondered if he'd gotten into some sort of financial difficulty. *Whatever the reason, it can't be easy for him to work for me.* The good thing was, a police car sitting outside was bound to scare off anyone bent on mischief making.

That being said, she hoped he didn't have a shift at the station the next morning, or justice might not have quite as much get-up-and-go as it usually did.

Back at the house, she thought she was finally going to get to go to bed, when she remembered that Chester and Houston were still out. At least she thought they were. First she went upstairs to check on Bonnie and found her sound asleep, her dark hair strewn across the pillow. Then she quietly knocked on each man's bedroom door. Getting no answer at either, she sighed and considered just leaving the front door unlocked so they could let themselves in. But if there was someone out there who had broken into the hall and was looking to cause trouble, might they take advantage of an unlocked door at the mansion?

She went back downstairs to the living room to retrieve a pillow and a throw before heading toward her office so she could recline on the old horsehair sofa that had been deposited there during the redecorating phase of the living room. Her office was right off the foyer, so she would hear if someone knocked on the front door. She'd leave on a light so they would see it through the window and know someone was nearby. She just hoped neither man would use the doorbell and wake the whole house.

As she entered the foyer, she heard muffled voices coming through the library doors. At first, she thought it was Chester and Houston, but the voices were too high-pitched. She put the pillow and throw in a chair, then walked to the huge double doors and pushed them open. Patricia and Florence stood facing one another across one of the library tables, looking like legendary archenemies. Patricia spoke angrily, and Florence wore a smirk that looked like a cat that had swallowed a canary. Patricia stopped in mid-sentence as the doors opened. Jillian figured that she must have been reading Florence the riot act, but the judge's reaction didn't seem appropriate to being dressed down.

"Sorry, ladies, I thought you had gone to bed." Jillian didn't know what else to say for a moment. It seemed lame now to say she was looking for the two men. "I'll just leave you two alone. I'll be in my office if you need anything." She closed the doors. Neither woman had attempted to say anything to her. Jillian retrieved her pillow and blanket and headed toward the office, thinking of the odd personalities currently sheltered under Belle Haven's roof.

It was just after midnight when she was awakened by an insistent knock on the front door. She opened it to find the bartender from Cap's, along with Chester and Houston. He had driven them home since they'd both had a bit too much "fun." She offered to tip the bartender, but he refused, saying that he'd already been compensated.

Just three more days and these people will be gone, she thought. *Monday night won't come soon enough.*

The next morning, just after six, Gooder was at the kitchen door to report it had been an uneventful night. He didn't look all that tired, and Jillian wondered if he'd slept a good part of the night. But as long as nothing had happened, she didn't mind. The police car itself was worth the price if it kept trouble away.

Bertie had already left for the bakery, and Cornelia asked Gooder in and offered him coffee and breakfast. He contentedly wolfed down a meal of buttermilk biscuits with sausage gravy, scrambled eggs, coffee, and orange juice before he left.

Not surprisingly, Houston didn't make as early an appearance as he had the previous morning, and when he did come downstairs, he spoke much more quietly than he had last night. He refused the biscuits and gravy, looking as though the very thought was repugnant. He avoided eye contact, pulled his hat forward to shade his eyes, and made no reference to his visit to Cap's. He just got himself a large cup of coffee and headed out the door toward the hall.

The other guests began to trickle into the breakfast area. They were mostly subdued, except for Florence, who seemed to be in high spirits, telling the others in a loud voice about how her local cooking show was soon to go national and her plans for writing a cookbook that was sure to be a best seller. Jillian had hoped to talk to Patricia privately about what Dorothea had told her about her spice labels being switched, but Patricia ate quickly and was out the door as soon as she finished. Jillian decided to go out to the hall and take Patricia aside to talk to her before filming began if she could.

Chester came downstairs still in his pajamas and robe, his long, gray hair uncombed and loose around his shoulders. Like Houston, he didn't seem terribly interested in having anything to do with traditional breakfast food. Squinting from the bright kitchen lights and wincing whenever Florence spoke, which was often, he asked for tomato juice plus Tabasco, Worcestershire sauce, horseradish, lemon juice, and a raw egg. He mixed the concoction, blending in salt, pepper, and several spices before drinking it down with a grimace. Jillian didn't see how it could possibly help his condition, but he seemed satisfied and headed back upstairs to shower and change.

Waldon was the last person to come down to join the others for breakfast. He was a sharp contrast to Chester, with his clothing perfectly pressed and every hair in place. He smelled of English Leather, the same aftershave Jillian's grandfather used to wear. He sat next to Avery, who commented on the scent. Apparently, she always bought it for her husband to wear as well. *Why am I not surprised?*

Jillian went upstairs while they finished eating to wake Bonnie and get her ready for the day. Then she fixed the child's breakfast and asked Cornelia to look after her while she went to talk to Patricia.

"Can I come with you, Miss Jillian?" Bonnie pleaded.

"Not for this, Bonnie," Jillian said. When the little girl's face fell, she added, "But I promise we'll have fun this afternoon. How does that sound?"

Bonnie perked right up. "Okay, Miss Jillian," she said amiably.

Jillian left the child chattering happily to Cornelia.

When she walked into Belle Haven Hall, Patricia was animatedly talking with Houston and Victor in a far corner of the room. Their faces looked serious, so Jillian decided to bide her time until they finished. In the meantime, she watched each baker getting things in order at his or her station. She noted that each counter held a footed, flat-bottomed, glass dish. Chester's and Kaylee's were the same shape, made of plain glass, so she guessed those had been provided for them, but the other three must have brought their own bowls from home. Avery's was a particularly beautiful cut-glass bowl that Jillian thought must be an antique.

Dorothea had said the recipe for that morning was to be a trifle—a mélange of sponge cake or cookies soaked with sherry or brandy, and layered with fresh fruit or jam, custard, and whipped cream. Jillian had seen recipes for nonalcoholic versions, but it looked like all of the contestants had either requested or brought their own favored brands of sherry or brandy.

She watched as Florence went from station to station. With a cameraman filming the exchange, she asked the bakers about the provenance of their recipes and about their "special" trifle ingredients. She received polite answers since she was, after all, one of the judges, and this was being filmed. Jillian wondered what it would have been like without the camera.

Florence came to Avery's station last. Avery's friendliness seemed the most genuine toward Florence. Jillian supposed that if what Kaylee had said about her being "aces" was accurate, perhaps she had not been as harshly criticized as the others and wasn't worried about her performance that day, so she was in a better mood.

Florence asked about Avery's bottle of sherry, which had large capital letters across the label. Avery bragged that she had ordered a case of the sherry from a company in Great Britain that boasted a Royal Warrant of appointment, as they were suppliers to the queen. When Florence asked to try a drop, Avery was clearly delighted to comply.

Florence put the small glass up to her lips and drained the mouthful that Avery had poured out, and Jillian looked to see if Patricia was free.

When she looked back, Florence was swaying, her breaths becoming short and shallow before she collapsed to the floor. Avery shouted for help and ran around her station to Florence's side as others converged on the spot. Jillian pulled out her phone and called 911.

A police car and an ambulance arrived within minutes. Jillian was relieved when it was Laura Lee who sprang out of the police car. Laura Lee instructed those gathered around to step away, and one of the EMTs knelt down to assess the patient. As he did, he asked questions about the circumstances before Florence's collapse. Jillian watched as he leaned forward to smell Florence's breath. She walked to the opposite side of Avery's station and leaned in to smell the sherry that remained in the bottle. It smelled like wine mixed with the slight hint of almond extract to her. She had a memory of something—a book or a movie—that had said there was a poison that smelled of bitter almonds, but she couldn't remember which poison it was.

They loaded Florence onto a stretcher and the EMT strapped an oxygen mask over her face. He pushed the stretcher toward the ambulance, speaking rapidly into his cell phone. He used a lot of jargon, but one word leaped out at Jillian: *Cyanide*.

After the ambulance left, Avery seemed more stunned than anything else, but several minutes later, she began to get rather agitated, her body shaking with tremors and tears in her eyes. She loudly proclaimed, "I did not try to poison anyone!" even though no one had accused her.

Waldon was near and put his arm around her shoulders to calm her. "No one suspects you of doing anything like that, Avery."

Avery seemed somewhat mollified by his comment. Unfortunately, Waldon didn't stop there.

"It seems likely to me that you were the real target, since bakers taste their food as they bake," he offered.

That seemed a likely scenario to Jillian too, but she wouldn't have said so right then seeing how near to hysteria Avery was.

Avery held her breath as realization dawned on her. Her eyes grew wide and tears that had gathered in her eyes poured down her cheeks. "That can't be!"

Waldon offered her his handkerchief and patted her shoulder, saying rather unhelpfully, "There, there."

Jillian's attention was drawn away as more members of law enforcement arrived, including the county sheriff, Coy Henderson. Jillian was glad to see him because he was a take-charge sort of person who brooked no nonsense and didn't make wild assumptions about guilt or innocence.

While the police began their work, Jillian scanned the faces of her other guests. Houston and Victor were grim, but Patricia was visibly shaken, and Victor had helped her to a chair. Kaylee was watching all the activity with sharp eyes, seeming to be more curious than sympathetic. Jillian thought this was a strange quality for a nurse. In fact, when Florence collapsed and Avery had shouted for help, Kaylee had not moved.

Chester had returned to his station and now seemed to be trying to minimize his presence. He appeared to be studying his stack of recipe cards, keeping his head down, but Jillian didn't believe for a moment that he was actually reading.

Dorothea was visibly shaking, so Jillian walked over to put her arm around her shoulders. She actually felt cold. *She's in shock.* Jillian looked around for something to cover her. Kaylee had a sweater folded on the shelf beneath the counter at her station.

"May I borrow that?" asked Jillian, pointing to the sweater.

Kaylee looked around. Her attention had been on Avery and Waldon. "Oh sure," she said when she understood Jillian's request and handed the sweater to her.

Dorothea put on the sweater and thanked Jillian. Kaylee had already gone back to watching the other activities in the room. Again, Jillian thought it strange behavior. The nurses she knew would have been looking out for ways they could help, not just watching with such detachment. Maybe it was because she was so young and new to the profession. *Still . . .*

After the forensics crew had finished, collecting not only Avery's bottle of sherry but all the other bottles as well, all present were advised that they were not to leave until the police had taken their statements. Sheriff Henderson set up an interview area in the unfinished kitchen, which could be closed off from the main area. Jillian was certain the pool of would-be poisoners would shortly be reduced to include only the people staying at Belle Haven since none of the crew would've had the opportunity to put cyanide in the bottle as far as she could tell.

Jillian asked Sheriff Henderson if she could give her statement first, which he granted. She told him briefly what had happened, but with so many people to get through, he didn't ask her many questions, meaning he didn't see her as a suspect. He told her that the police would need to search the house, and she gave her permission in general, knowing he would have to get each guest's permission to search their personal belongings unless he had a warrant.

At the end of the interview, she got his leave to run up to the mansion to let Cornelia know what was going on. She had no doubt seen the flashing lights and heard the sirens. Jillian also wanted to check on Bonnie to explain their time together that afternoon might have to be postponed.

She met Cornelia on the path, halfway from the house, walking toward the hall.

"Where's Bonnie?"

Cornelia's tone was impatient. "She's fine. Maudie and Wanda Jean are here this morning to help out again. We want to know what's going on."

Jillian explained what had happened as they walked toward the house. She thought of the reason she had gone out to the hall in the first place—to talk to Patricia about the attempted sabotage on Dorothea the day before.

Switched labels on spice bottles seemed like small potatoes now.

If Jillian had thought the previous evening radiated bad vibes, it was nothing compared to the atmosphere that settled over Belle Haven with the knowledge that it was likely that one among them had poisoned Florence. They eyed each other with suspicion. The guests didn't even trust their hosts. Most declined to eat from the lunch buffet that had been prepared, preferring to go into town. Sheriff Henderson had approved it, warning all that no one was to leave the environs of Moss Hollow.

That afternoon, all the rooms had been searched by the police, making everyone even less at ease. Avery was the most cautious of all. She distanced herself from everyone except Waldon, with whom she'd been the friendliest anyway. Jillian couldn't blame her. It appeared that someone in the house had actually wished *her* harm, rather than Florence. Jillian was rather surprised that Avery chose to remain at Belle Haven at all, though there weren't many choices of hotel in Moss Hollow proper. The Southern Peach Inn was probably full with the TV production crew in residence, and since it was Saturday, any of the remaining accommodations would likely be taken.

Attendance at supper that evening was even slimmer than it had been the night before—the only ones who had stayed in were Patricia, Victor, and Dorothea, who all sat together in the dining room.

Just before the meal was served, the landline phone in the kitchen rang. Jillian answered. It was Laura Lee, calling from the hospital with some welcome news.

"Florence has been given the antidote for cyanide," said Laura Lee. "She's expected to recover completely and should be released from the hospital in just a couple of days. Apparently it was a very small dose."

"That is wonderful news. I'll pass it along to the others. That should give at least a little bit of comfort. Were any of the other bottles of sherry poisoned?"

"Looks like Avery's bottle was the only one that had been tampered with."

"Is there anything we can do for Florence?"

"Not that I know of. We called her husband. He's already at the hospital with his wife."

"Why don't you give him my number and tell him to call if he needs anything?" Jillian offered.

"That would be great, Jillian. Thank you."

"Thanks for calling us to let us know how she's doing."

Someone in the background called Laura Lee's name. She said a few words to the person and then returned to Jillian. "I've got to go. I'll see you tomorrow afternoon if you're not too tied up to come to the Sweetie Pies meeting."

She hung up before Jillian could reply.

Jillian relayed the information after they were all seated at the dining table, and some awkward conversation followed. After that, there was a long period of silence while they ate. Even Bonnie was quiet. Jillian hadn't told her any details of what had happened, only that Florence, whom Bonnie had dubbed "the loud lady," had become ill and been taken to the hospital. Even so, the little girl seemed to understand that something was not right, preferring to watch the grown-ups with big blue eyes rather than eating her meal. Jillian had to remind her several times about the food in front of her.

Jillian looked for some topic of conversation that would bring some normality back to the situation. "Patricia, how did you come to write *Blissful Baking*? Were you a professional baker?"

Patricia smiled, but it seemed rather sad. "No, not at all." She took a deep breath as if deciding whether or not to share. "In 1968, I was newly widowed. I had two small children and no marketable skills. It was only after my husband's death that I found out how dire our financial situation was. We'd been living very well. We had a lovely home and a new car. We ate out at the best restaurants and took fabulous vacations overseas. I had no idea that we were so deeply in debt.

"The only thing I really knew how to do was to keep house and look after our children. I enjoyed being a homemaker, especially cooking and baking, and in my desperation to provide for my children, I came up with the idea that I could produce a cookbook for bakers. Knowing more about the business world now, I realize it was naïve of me to think I could succeed, but I suppose my ignorance was a good thing then—blissful, you might say. As it happened, Albert—that was my husband—and I were good friends with a man named Greg who worked at a well-known publishing house in Boston. I approached him with the idea, and I have to say my presentation was good. He thought so too, and he agreed to publish the book. Sadly, he passed away a couple of years ago, but I still publish with the same company. I must say it's been a good and lucrative relationship through all of these years."

"I didn't know you'd been through all that, Patricia," said Victor. He smiled. "You must have been pretty spunky."

That made Patricia laugh, something Jillian had rarely seen her do in the short time she'd known her. "No one has ever called me 'spunky' before. I guess I was, but it felt more like controlled terror talking to those business types. But I did it because I was determined to take care of my children, and I learned a lot along the way."

"How did your TV show come about?" asked Cornelia.

"Oh, that was another fluke. Part of my contract with the publishing company was that I had to do book signings and appear on whatever TV and radio shows would have me to advertise the book. Greg arranged for me to do a baking segment on a local morning show. A TV producer from a different channel saw it and contacted me, asking if I wanted to do a pilot, with the hope of a twelve-episode series. It was to be filmed in town, so it was ideal for me, and provided an income while we waited to see what the sales would be like for *Blissful Baking*."

"And both the cookbook and TV show took off," said Victor. "Well done."

"I think it was just dumb luck," Patricia said humbly.

"More likely hard work," said Bertie.

"That too," she said with a smile.

There was silence for a couple of minutes before Dorothea quietly asked the question on everyone's mind. "What's going to happen with our show?"

Patricia sighed. "I don't know. We obviously can't go on until this is solved, and even then . . ."

"But we already have five episodes in the can," said Victor. "Surely there's something we can do."

Patricia shrugged helplessly. "If there is, I don't know what it is right now. We'll have to wait and see what the police discover, and by then, I doubt our contestants will be interested in hanging around. And I don't blame them. Our other episodes went so smoothly. This one almost seems to be cursed."

At the word "cursed," Jillian sent a sideways glance at Aunt Cornelia, whose mouth had opened slightly as if she were about to speak. Afraid she was about to say something about the so-called "ghostly" happenings in the barn, Jillian was ready to jump in until she saw one of those familiar twin-sister looks pass between

Bertie and Cornelia. This time it was, more precisely, a look of communication from Bertie to Cornelia. Cornelia closed her mouth and didn't say a word.

Jillian was sound asleep in bed when she felt a little hand on her arm. A sweet voice whispered, "Miss Jillian?" The hand patted her arm gently. "Miss Jillian."

Jillian opened one eye to see Bonnie kneeling next to her on the bed, leaning over her. "What is it, Bonnie?"

"I can't sleep."

Jillian's first thought was a mental groan, but she kept it to herself. Then she began to feel thankful for this little bit of gentle normality in the face of what had happened earlier in the day. "Are you feeling okay?" She raised herself up and felt the little girl's forehead. It didn't seem especially warm.

"I am a little thirsty."

Jillian looked at the clock. It was one thirty. "Would you like a glass of water?" She sat up, ready to pour a glass from the carafe she kept on the nightstand.

"Could I have some cocoa instead?"

"Won't that keep you awake?"

"Mama fixes me cocoa sometimes when I can't sleep."

Bonnie hadn't mentioned her parents since Friday, when they had called to let her know they had safely arrived in Washington after a five-day drive across country. Though they had assured her it would only be a few more days before Lilith would return to Georgia to pick her up, Jillian wondered if Bonnie was starting to feel a little homesick for her parents. *It must seem like a long time to a five-year-old.* Jillian got out of bed and pulled her bathrobe over her light cotton nightgown. "I guess we'd better have some cocoa then."

Bonnie laughed and clapped her hands once.

"Shh." Jillian put her index finger to her lips. "We have to be very quiet so we don't wake up anyone else."

"Okay."

After Jillian first gathered and then pulled her long red hair out from inside her bathrobe, she helped Bonnie put on her bathrobe and did the same with her long black hair, thinking as she did so that they had equally messy bed head. But it didn't matter. It wasn't like anyone would see them at that hour. Then she rummaged in the drawers for a pair of socks for each of them. She was afraid their slippers would be too noisy, but the floors in Belle Haven were usually cold, even during the hottest days of summer.

It was a bright moonlit night. Light streamed down through the stained glass dome over the stairs, so they didn't need the small flashlight Jillian had grabbed from her nightstand drawer. She stuck it in her pocket, and they made it to the kitchen without incident. Jillian turned on the light over the sink instead of the bright overhead, while Bonnie climbed up on a stool at the kitchen island.

It didn't take long for Jillian to warm up some milk on the stove and add some premade cocoa mix before pouring it into a couple of small mugs. She placed a steaming mug in front of Bonnie and sat down next to her. "Be careful. It's hot."

Bonnie blew across the top a few times before taking a sip. "Will you read me a story when we're finished?"

"Maybe just a short one, and then we have to go back to bed. Okay?"

Bonnie smiled. "Okay."

"I'll read you one of the short stories from *Grimm's Fairy*

Tales. Would you like me to read 'Snow White' to you?" That seemed to be a favorite story of Bonnie's as she often mentioned seeing the ballet.

"Yes, please."

When they'd finished, Jillian rinsed the mugs and then took Bonnie's hand to lead the way to the library where she'd left the books she'd found in the attic. Here she needed the flashlight, which she shined toward the table where she'd left the books. Not seeing them, she flashed the light further afield. Still no sign. She reached over to turn on a table lamp and then turned off the flashlight and stashed it back in her pocket.

"I could have sworn I put them on this table," she muttered to herself. "Bonnie, will you help me find the books we looked at when you first came? But remember to be quiet. We don't want to wake up anyone, especially not Miss Bertie."

"Okay. I'll be very quiet," she whispered. She began walking on her tiptoes around the room peering over the edges of tables and running her hand along shelves she could reach. She looked at her hand and scrunched up her nose. "It's dusty in here."

Jillian couldn't help but chuckle. "I'm afraid you're right."

"I could help dust, Miss Jillian. I do it at home all the time. Mama says I'm the best duster there is."

"I just might take you up on that. But not tonight."

They continued looking for several minutes before it occurred to Jillian to ask Bonnie a more pointed question. After all, what was it they said about children? *Little pictures have big eyes?* No. That didn't make sense. *Ah. Little pitchers have big ears. That's it.* Whatever the case, she might know something. "Bonnie, have you seen anyone with the books or heard anyone talk about them?"

Bonnie thought a moment. "The loud lady—"

She was interrupted by a piercing *crack* from somewhere outside. Two more sounded in close succession.

Jillian thought, *Were those gunshots?* "Bonnie, come with me, quick."

"But what about the books?"

Jillian placed her hands on Bonnie's shoulders to hurry her along. "We'll look later."

"What was that noise?"

"I'm not sure." She didn't want to say.

They met Bertie just coming out of her bedroom on the way back to the living room where Jillian had intended to ensconce Bonnie on the sofa before going outside to investigate.

"Did you hear that?" asked Jillian in a low voice.

"I did. What are you two doing down here?"

Jillian tried to keep her voice calm for Bonnie's sake. "Just having a little midnight snack. Will you watch her while I run out and see what that was?"

Bertie looked doubtful. "Don't you think you should leave it to Gooder?"

"But what if . . .?" She didn't want to finish the sentence.

"Oh all right."

Jillian turned to leave.

"Wait!"

Bertie disappeared inside her bedroom and then reappeared with a heavy wooden cane that had a thick knob on one end instead of a hook. She handed it to Jillian. "Just in case."

Jillian accepted the cane and nodded. She headed toward the back door while Bertie herded Bonnie toward the staircase.

"It's time you were in bed," said Bertie.

"But Miss Jillian was going to read me a story."

"I'll tell you one after you get back into bed. Let's go."

"Do you know any stories?"

Bertie harrumphed. "Of course. I know lots of stories."

"Why does Miss Jillian call you Bertie instead of Grandma?"

"Because that's what I want her to call me."

"Don't you like being a grandma?"

"Don't be foolish, child. Of course I do."

Jillian couldn't hear the rest of the conversation as Bertie and Bonnie were further away and she had reached the back door, but she thought that, perhaps, the formidable Bertie had finally met her match.

On the back porch, Jillian stuck her feet in an old pair of rubber boots that Cornelia kept there for when she was gardening. They were meant to be worn over shoes, so they were several sizes too large for her feet. They flopped as she tried to run down the path in the moonlight toward the old barn, slowing her down considerably. When she was closer, she saw Gooder outside shining a large flashlight in the tall grass along the overgrown fencerow.

"Gooder! Are you all right? Were those gunshots?"

He turned the flashlight directly on her, which blinded her, so she turned her head slightly and put her forearm up over her eyes, still clutching the cane. "Do you mind?"

He waited a few moments before he turned the flashlight back toward the fencerow.

"Well, aren't you going to say anything?"

He seemed in no hurry to reply, but kept flashing the light back and forth, obviously looking for something—or somebody. She moved next to him and saw that he held his pistol in his other hand. Suddenly he froze.

Jillian's gaze followed the beam into the low brush that shook as if the wind was whipping it back and forth, but there was no wind. Something was moving through the thick grass and weeds. It was something very large, but low to the ground. She remembered reading an article about pet pythons being released into the wild by owners that no longer wanted to care for them. Was it some sort of giant snake moving not fifteen feet away from them? She wanted to run, but her feet felt frozen in place by fear. She gripped the cane tighter and stepped a little behind Gooder. He glanced at her, but said nothing.

Finally, whatever it was reached a large, old, gnarly tree that had grown into the old fence. She was prepared to see a snake begin to slither up the trunk. The brush shuddered and so did she. She felt a scream building in her lungs.

But when she saw what it was, she laughed out loud with relief instead.

Two baby raccoons began to climb the tree. These were followed by another, and another, and another. In the end, five raccoons, each just a little smaller than Possum, climbed in a spiral around the tree, their eyes glowing yellow in the beam of light.

"There are your burglars," said Gooder, his shoulders relaxing.

"And you shot at them?"

"Well, I was dozing slightly, and they surprised me. I heard noises outside and, when I came out, just saw glowing eyes, so I shot a couple of rounds in the air to scare them off."

"Do you think you can catch them?"

Gooder snorted. "Me? No way. That is not in my job description. They may be cute to look at, but they're vicious if you corner them. The mama's probably around here somewhere too, and she's probably twice as big and twice as mean as these. You're going to have to get someone else to do that."

"Like who?"

"I don't know, maybe county animal control. They could probably send someone out in a week or so."

"A week or so? I can't wait that long. With what happened this morning . . ." Her words trailed off. She really did not want to talk about that with Gooder.

"I heard about that. You just can't stay out of trouble, can you?"

"It's not my fault."

"It never is." His tone was resigned. "Do you want me to stay on tonight or not?"

"Well, yes, I want you to stay. There'll have to be someone here at least until I figure out how to get rid of all these raccoons."

"I could shoot 'em."

"You will do no such thing!"

"Your choice." He put his gun back in his holster and looked over at Jillian. "You'd better get inside. You're not really dressed for outdoors."

Jillian had forgotten that she was in her nightgown and bathrobe. She looked down at them blowing around her legs. How had she not noticed that the hem was coming loose? And those boots were ridiculous. Looking a mess in front of Gooder Jones had never been high on her to-do list. She turned on her heel and clomped back toward the house, painfully aware that she was losing dignity with every rubbery step.

"Good night, Jillian." He sounded amused.

She did not reply.

When the alarm went off Sunday morning, Jillian considered skipping church. She almost wished she'd turned off the alarm when she came back to bed after explaining to Bertie about the raccoons. Bertie laughed and said she wanted to be the one to tell Cornelia. That sounded like trouble to Jillian, but she was too tired to argue about it.

She stayed in bed, thinking about what to do. She'd missed church last Sunday, so she supposed she should go this week. The alarm didn't seem to have disturbed Bonnie, so Jillian decided to leave her asleep for now.

As soon as she stepped into the hallway, she could smell the aroma of coffee and bacon drifting up from downstairs. She breathed deeply and headed downstairs. In the kitchen, Bertie was at the stove turning what looked to be the second or third batch of bacon, as there were already several pieces draining on a platter lined with paper towels. Jillian grabbed a strip and took a bite. *Ah, bacon, the food of the gods—after chocolate.*

A piece broke off and fell to the floor. She didn't have to bother to pick it up. Possum was at her feet already and took care of it. He sat down and looked up expectantly, waiting for another morsel to fall his way.

"It appears the two people who got the least amount of sleep last night are the first two up," said Jillian as she grabbed a mug for coffee.

"Don't forget about Gooder. He was already in here this morning."

"And I suppose you fed him."

"I did. It was a small price to pay to get his account of the raccoon caper."

"Very funny."

"What's funny?" Cornelia walked through the kitchen door and made a beeline to the bacon. Before she took a bite, she broke off a substantial piece and gave it to Possum.

Bertie looked at Jillian with a cocked eyebrow. "Shall I tell her now?"

Jillian rolled her eyes. "I suppose so." She grabbed another piece of bacon and took her coffee cup with her as she left the kitchen to head back upstairs for a shower.

Jillian had extended an invitation to all the guests to attend Moss Hollow Fellowship Church with them when they first arrived at Belle Haven. Only Patricia and Dorothea said they planned to attend. Victor left earlier to go to nearby Painter's Ridge to attend the Catholic church—with the permission of Sheriff Henderson—and Avery and Waldon said they were going to the Episcopalian church across town. Just before it was time to leave for church, Jillian found Chester and Houston together in the library, where they were both reading. There had been no sign of Kaylee that morning, so Jillian assumed she was sleeping in.

With Bonnie's car seat, it was too crowded for all of them to ride to church together in Jillian's car, so Dorothea drove her car with Patricia as her passenger. Jillian led the way, eventually driving up the lane to the impressive old church with its square pillars and white siding where it sat perched on a hilltop. The parking lot seemed fuller than usual when they arrived, so it took some time before she found a parking spot.

Each Sunday, a volunteer or two were assigned to greet churchgoers as they entered the church. This week it was Annalise Reed, another member of the Sweetie Pies, and her husband, Byron, who was vice president at the local bank.

After Jillian had introduced the Reeds to Bonnie, Annalise put her hand on Jillian's arm and leaned in close. "Maudie and Wanda Jean told me what happened at Belle Haven yesterday. Did your guest, you know, uh . . .?" She looked at Bonnie with a strained smile before looking back at Jillian. "I mean to say, is she okay?"

"Fortunately, yes. She's recovering at the hospital."

Annalise shook her head. "You poor thing. You have the worst luck."

Jillian didn't know what to say to that. "Well, not as bad as some." *Like Florence, for instance.*

Patricia and Dorothea had followed Cornelia and Bertie to the pew near the front where members of the Belle family had sat for decades. She glanced to one side and saw Hunter Greyson sitting alone. She hadn't seen him in a week, and she was surprised by how long that suddenly felt. He looked so handsome wearing a navy-blue suit and bright-blue tie that matched the color of his eyes. His dark hair, streaked with the occasional gray, had curled slightly in the muggy Georgia heat outside.

He had noticed Jillian at the same time and stood up, smiling. It just made him all the more handsome.

"Who's your friend?" he asked, looking at Bonnie. His inquiry was a ruse, as Jillian had told him that she would be babysitting all week, and perhaps a bit longer, which now looked to be the case. Lilith had called the night before and asked if Bonnie could impose on their hospitality a few more days, as they'd run into a few snafus with the move. The Belle Haven women had assured her it wouldn't be a problem, and they meant it.

"Hunter Greyson, I'd like you to meet Bonnie Trueblood, my cousin."

He gently shook Bonnie's hand, his own dwarfing hers. "I'm pleased to meet you, Bonnie. Would you girls care to sit with me this morning?"

"What do you think, Bonnie? Shall we?" Jillian asked.

The little girl looked between the two grown-ups with a discerning eye. "Is he your boyfriend?"

Jillian felt warmth rush into her face and was sure it was turning bright red.

Hunter grinned. "Well, I'm a boy, and we are very good friends."

"Have you kissed her?"

Jillian heard several people snicker in the row in front and behind them. Fortunately, the organ began to play, signaling it was time to be seated and prepare for the beginning of the service.

"Bonnie, let's sit down."

Hunter moved over and Bonnie sat between him and Jillian. Bonnie looked up toward Hunter. "You can tell me the answer when church is over," she whispered loudly enough to be heard over the music. Jillian heard more snickers from the surrounding pews.

After Jillian had settled in, marking the location of the first hymn with her bulletin, she looked ahead a few rows and saw Savannah and James sitting together. They seemed to spend a lot of time together, and Jillian knew that they were more than old friends who enjoyed each other's company. But her best friend sparingly shared information about their relationship. *Time will tell*, she thought. *Or I guess I could sic Bonnie on them—she'd get to the bottom of it.* The thought made her smile.

A few rows ahead on the other side of the aisle sat Lenora Ryan, who was more than just the linchpin of the bakery. It was Lenora who'd had the patience to help Jillian learn to bake after she came back to Georgia. Whenever Jillian had been ready to give up, Lenora gave her not only practical advice, but encouragement. Now Jillian could hold her own in the bakery. She'd learned so much in a short time, and a lot of that was thanks to Lenora.

Lenora lived alone, having been widowed many years ago. She had sold her house just a short time before Jillian returned to Georgia, in order to help her daughter go back to school. Lenora had been living in the apartment above the bakery since then. She usually sat with her sister's family on Sunday morning, but today she was in the company of her daughter, Dorie, Dorie's husband, Abram, and their son, Henry, who were visiting from Alabama.

When church had ended, Bonnie looked at Hunter with the expectation that he would tell her whether or not he had kissed Jillian, but he deflected by saying he would stop by Belle Haven before she left and they'd have a talk in private. Bonnie seemed to like that idea, so they said goodbye to Hunter, who explained he couldn't stay for Sunday school because he needed to prepare for a viewing at the funeral home that afternoon.

Jillian could tell by Bonnie's puzzled expression that she was about to launch into a series of questions about what a viewing was. To head her off, she took the little girl by the hand and went against the flow of people in the center aisle to introduce her to Savannah and James. It turned out they weren't staying for Sunday school either as they had plans to go to an art show in Marietta.

"Is that this weekend? I was going to go to that this year. Rats. I even marked it on my purse calendar so I wouldn't forget. Not that I could get away now. I guess it will have to wait until next year."

"It's understandable that you're a bit distracted with everything that's going on," Savannah said kindly.

"Oh, you heard about that."

"Maudie and Wanda Jean."

"Of course." Jillian sighed and looked around. "Well, I don't want to keep you. Y'all have fun."

Savannah leaned in and lowered her voice. "Do you need me to stick around for moral support? We don't have to go."

Jillian would have liked nothing better, but she couldn't be that selfish with her friend. "No. You two go and have a good time. Maybe we can talk tomorrow. Perhaps we'll have some answers by then."

Savannah smiled and patted her friend's arm. "I hope so."

Jillian began to guide Bonnie toward the Sunday school room for her age group when she met up with Dorie and Henry headed the same direction.

"Hi, Jillian," said Dorie. "How are you?"

They hugged as Jillian said, "I'm okay, I think."

"Yeah, I heard about what happened."

"Let me guess. Maudie and Wanda Jean."

Dorie laughed. "Wanda Jean called Mom last evening, so technically, it was just her."

Jillian leaned in. "It wouldn't surprise me if they made lists and split up names to let everyone in Moss Hollow know."

After more chitchat, during which she introduced Bonnie, Jillian asked if she could take Henry to the classroom. Dorie agreed, telling Henry to look out for the younger girl. Though he was only a year older than Bonnie, he was a few inches taller and, being a boy, he was heftier. Following his mother's instructions, Henry took Bonnie's little hand in his slightly larger one, and the two of them followed Jillian side by side. Having been in the company of only adults for a week, Bonnie seemed thrilled to be with another child.

"I've never been to this Sunday school before," said Bonnie. "Is the teacher nice?"

"I've only been here a couple of times," answered Henry, "but the teacher was nice last time."

"Don't you live 'round here?"

"No, I'm from Alabama."

"I don't think I've ever been to Al'bama. But I'm going to move to Wash'ton state soon."

"Where's that?"

"It's far, far away."

"Like in *Star Wars*?"

"Where's that?"

"It's not a place—it's a movie my dad and I watch sometimes. Haven't you ever seen it?"

"No. I like movies with princesses."

"*Star Wars* has a princess."

"It does? It must be okay then, but I'll have to ask my mama."

They had reached the classroom door. Jillian said, "I'll meet you back here when Sunday school is over." She watched through the glass in the door as they took a seat next to each other at one of the small tables. As they continued to talk with solemn little faces, she thought she would have liked to have been a fly on the wall to listen in on the rest of that conversation. Between the church service and this innocent interaction, she'd almost forgotten the problems that awaited her at home.

When they arrived back at Belle Haven, a police car was parked in front of the house. As they turned to drive up the lane, Laura Lee stepped out of the car, in uniform and looking very serious. Jillian hoped she was merely striking the pose of her office and was not the bearer of bad tidings. Perhaps Florence had taken a turn for the worse.

Jillian stopped her car in the porte cochere while Dorothea pulled hers into the front loop behind the police car. Jillian helped Bonnie out of the car, instructing her to follow Bertie and Cornelia into the house while she went up front to talk to Laura Lee.

Laura Lee was already speaking with Patricia as Jillian approached. It didn't look good. She saw Dorothea walking up the steps toward the front door of the house, looking back at the police car every few steps. Then Laura Lee opened the back door of her patrol car and assisted Patricia inside.

"What's going on?" asked Jillian as she drew near. Houston had opened the front door and stepped out on the veranda, followed by Chester, Kaylee, and Dorothea.

Laura Lee looked at Jillian after she closed the car door. "I've been instructed to take her in for questioning."

"Is she under arrest?"

"Not yet."

"What do you mean, 'not yet'? Is there some new evidence?"

Laura Lee lowered her voice. "I can't say much, but Florence has given a statement accusing Patricia of trying to kill her because she 'knows the truth' about something in Patricia's past."

"Like what?"

"She won't say yet. But, according to her, it's something that Patricia would do anything to keep quiet, including murder."

After lunch was over, Bertie and Cornelia headed over to the Chocolate Shoppe for the Southern Sweetie Pies meeting that was held there most Sunday afternoons. Jillian could have taken Bonnie too, but she had stayed behind using the excuse that Bonnie was probably tired from being up in the middle of the night and needed a nap. The real reason was that she hoped to get a nap herself that afternoon. Bonnie hadn't been taking naps since she'd been at Belle Haven, but Jillian was hoping that today would be the exception. Between the weight of having strangers in the house, the attempt on Florence's life, and the events of last night, she was exhausted. Closing her eyes for an hour or so would feel like heaven.

She had just finished putting the last few things from lunch in the dishwasher when the phone rang in the kitchen. It was Florence's husband, Charles Oglethorpe, calling from the hospital. His tone was less than cordial.

"I'll be coming by to pick up Florence's things this afternoon around three. Please have them ready to go."

"If you need a place to stay while Florence recovers, you're welcome to stay at Belle Haven."

"I wouldn't dream of staying in such a place. Florence has told me of the disgraceful treatment she received there before this near-tragedy occurred. You just have her bags at the front door ready for me to collect as soon as I get there. I want to spend as little time as possible under your roof."

Jillian wanted to ask what "disgraceful treatment" he was referring to, but let it slide. The man was no doubt stressed, a condition she well understood. She replied in as even a tone as she could muster, "I'll have her things ready and waiting at three o'clock."

"See that you do. Florence says her suitcase, shoe bag, and hanging bag are ready to go. The only thing you need to do is to put her nightclothes and toiletries in the smaller bag. She'll know if anything is missing, so don't try to pull anything. We don't want to have to call our lawyer about your establishment, but be assured we won't hesitate to do so."

Without another word, he hung up. She shook her head, staring at the phone in her hand. "Some people." She placed the handset back in the cradle. She had intended to ask him about Florence's car, but he hadn't given her a chance. She would have to ask when he arrived to retrieve the luggage. She walked over to the table in the breakfast nook to sit down and think, but it wasn't an easy thing to do when she was steaming about the implications of his words. To make wild claims about her "treatment" at Belle Haven, then accuse her of even thinking of stealing any of his wife's things was so ridiculous she couldn't even fathom his mind-set. From what she knew of Florence, Charles Oglethorpe appeared to be her perfect match.

Patricia had called this TV episode "cursed." It was sounding more and more like that was an apt description.

After Florence was taken to the hospital, it had seemed obvious to Jillian that Avery must have been the intended victim, and she had wondered why someone would want to harm Avery. But now, was it a given that Avery was the target? The police didn't seem to think so.

But the police were sometimes wrong. For some reason, she thought of Gooder and was glad Laura Lee had come to pick up Patricia instead.

At any rate, Florence's accusation could just be a detour from the truth. She didn't doubt that Florence would do anything to keep the attention on herself. *So,* she reasoned, *if Avery was the one who was meant to ingest the poison, was it possible that another one of the contestants had done this to get rid of the front-runner?* Jillian didn't have any idea what the ultimate prize for winning was, but she didn't think it could be much more than being named something like Best Baker in America, which seemed a pretty weak motive for attempted murder.

And how could the assailant be so cavalier? Putting poison in a bottle like that—several people could have been affected or even died. Perhaps they were dealing with a psychopath, someone with no regard for the safety or well-being of others. That was frightening.

She circled back around to the current state of affairs. The police thought that Patricia might be the culprit, and Florence had been the intended victim. In the short time she'd known Patricia, it just didn't seem possible to Jillian that she could have done this, no matter what information about her past Florence thought she. had. The act itself seemed counterproductive to Patricia's goals, since it was now doubtful that the show could even go on.

Then she remembered the argument she'd witnessed between Patricia and Florence in the library. Could that exchange have contained the reason that might cause Patricia to poison the judge she had hired? Jillian now wished she'd eavesdropped a little.

Nothing was making sense. Jillian sifted other details through her mind. Would Avery have tasted the sherry before she used it? If she had a case at home as she said, it seemed probable that she had already tasted a bottle of the sherry and had approved its flavor for her trifle. Perhaps it really was more likely that Florence was the target. But it could have been Victor as well, since he also would have tasted Avery's trifle in order to judge it.

Jillian had spoken very little with Victor. On his infomercials he seemed like a brash Chicagoan to her, but in real life, she had found him to be rather quiet and polite. Was it possible that he might have an enemy among her guests? Or was he the villain? There was certainly no love lost between him and Florence. Could he have poisoned the bottle to get rid of his co-judge?

Every possibility she could come up with seemed as unlikely as the next, if for no other reason than each one jeopardized the whole production. Besides, if Victor wanted Florence out, as the judge who appeared in every episode, Jillian presumed he would have enough clout to ask Patricia to simply fire her. And as producer Patricia could just fire Florence outright if she had a problem with her. Attempting murder was an extreme and unnecessary option for any of the scenarios Jillian could come up with. Something else was going on, but Jillian couldn't put her finger on what.

Jillian's head began to ache, and she rubbed her temples with her fingers to try to relieve some of the tension she was feeling. She really needed that nap.

Bonnie wandered in from where she'd been playing in the living room. "Miss Jillian? Will you come and play with me?"

Jillian's mind was so full of thoughts and confusion about the current situation that she didn't respond, but just closed her eyes to try to organize her thoughts into something useful.

Bonnie pulled on her sleeve. "Miss Jillian, would you—"

"Bonnie, please be quiet! I'm trying to think." Her tone was harsh. She might as well have told the child to shut up. The words were out before she could stop herself, and she immediately felt terrible, especially seeing the shocked look on the little girl's face.

"Oh, Bonnie, I'm so sorry. I didn't mean to snap at you. It's just that I'm worried, but that's not your fault, and I shouldn't have taken it out on you. Will you forgive me?"

"Yes, Miss Jillian."

But Jillian could see in the girl's expression that something had changed in that moment. She felt as if she'd broken a piece of antique china she could never put back together. When she reached out to touch her arm, the little girl pulled away.

"Tell you what. I think we're both a little tired since we were up so late last night. How about if I read you a story?"

"But we don't know where the books are." Her voice was small, and she kept her head down rather than look at Jillian.

"No, but we could read another chapter of *A Little Princess*, and there are other books in the library."

Bonnie was still a little standoffish, but agreed in a somber tone. Jillian decided a lighter story was called for and grabbed an old picture book from the library that had been one of her favorites as a child. Bonnie held onto the rail instead of Jillian's hand as they went upstairs to Jillian's bedroom. In bed, she cradled Mr. Benjamin in her arms, yawning periodically as she listened to the adventures of Bill the crocodile and his "toothbrush" bird friend, Pete. Not long after Jillian closed the book, Bonnie was asleep.

Jillian closed her eyes too, but soon her mind began to race again with more thoughts about the poisoning and who had done what to whom, asking herself why nothing was making any sense. She couldn't stay settled. She opened her eyes and glanced at the clock. *Two o'clock.* She had to make sure Florence's belongings were ready to go when Charles arrived, so she slowly got up, leaving Bonnie asleep on the bed.

She hadn't been in the bedroom where Florence had stayed since the police had done a search after the crime. Florence had left a pair of shoes under a chair. Jillian found a shoe bag nearby, put the shoes inside, and placed it next to the door. In the closet, Florence's hanging bag was zipped up, so she took it out and laid it across the bed. It took her less than a minute to deposit Florence's toiletries and makeup in the small bag Charles had mentioned and to fold Florence's nightgown and place it in the zippered side pocket on the same bag. She looked around the room for anything else that didn't belong at Belle Haven. She found an eyeshadow palette in outrageous shades of purple, red, and even vivid green on the bedside table. She was pretty sure that could only belong to Florence. She stuffed it in the small bag.

The lid to Florence's suitcase was closed, but not zipped. It was lying on a folding luggage holder Jillian had placed in the room. She started to zip it up, but stopped and decided to take one more look in the closet, remembering Charles's threat of calling his lawyer if anything was missing. Florence had worn chunky costume jewelry, but it didn't appear to be anything that was terribly valuable. What was he so worried about?

She opened the closet door, and sure enough, a silky jersey tunic that had bright neon-orange and -pink stripes had slipped off a hanger and was lying on the floor. She knew it didn't belong to anyone who lived at Belle Haven. She folded it neatly on the bed and then took it to the suitcase to put it inside.

After she opened the lid, she wasn't surprised to find clothing covered with large prints and stripes in eye-catching colors of bright reds, oranges, hot pinks, and purples. She put the tunic inside and was about to close the suitcase when something caught her eye, mainly for the mellowness of its butter-yellow color. With one finger she pushed aside the garments that covered it. Florence had hidden the old British flour-mill company booklet that Jillian had found in the attic in her suitcase. Why would she try to steal that? What was that woman up to?

Bonnie woke from her nap when she heard the click of Jillian closing the door behind her, having not really reached a deep sleep. She was sad and homesick. "Mama doesn't yell at me like that." She hugged Mr. Benj'min and cried a little. "Why don't Mama and Daddy come and get me? I want to go home."

She lay there for several moments, feeling very sorry for herself. She sat up and looked around the room, her gaze settling on the book A Little Princess, on Jillian's nightstand. She got up with a determination to find the other books. "Then maybe Miss Jillian won't be upset with me anymore."

In her stocking feet, she left the room, carrying Mr. Benj'min with her. She quietly closed the door behind her and tiptoed down the stairs. She peeked around the library door where Mr. Houston, the man with the funny hat, and Mr. Chester, the man with the ponytail, were playing a game with cards. They talked and laughed about things she didn't understand. She didn't think the books she was looking for were in there. She and Miss Jillian didn't find them last night, and she'd seen the loud lady, Miss Florence, take the yellow book away. That book didn't look like it would have good stories, so she wasn't worried about finding it. She didn't see the loud lady take any of the other books, but someone else could have.

Behind her, she heard the front door creak as someone pushed to open it, and a man's voice saying something about his "Aunt Teek's writing set." She recognized the voice as belonging to Mr. Waldon, the man who gave her a mean look when she asked him a question. She didn't like him at all.

She just barely found a hiding place behind the door in Jillian's office before he stepped into the foyer. She peeked through the crack between the door and the doorframe to see that he was with Miss Avery, who called her "poppet" whenever she spoke to her. Bonnie waited and listened for a little while. Their voices *eventually faded when she heard the sound of footsteps going up the staircase.*

She checked the main floor, moving furtively from room to room. There didn't seem to be anyone else there. There was no sign of Miss Jillian, or of Miss Bertie or Miss Cornel'a. She looked in all the places she could think of where she might put the books if she wanted to hide them. She was pretty good at hide-and-seek, but it didn't seem to be helping her find the books so far. She decided to go up the stairs to the second floor. The hallway was empty, so she figured that most of the baking people were in their rooms, except for the ones she'd already seen.

She thought about asking Miss Dorothea to help her. She was nice. But Miss Dorothea hadn't seemed to feel very well lately, so she decided not to bother her. Miss Kaylee reminded her of the babysitters that stayed with her at home when her parents went out. She was all right, but she wasn't sure which room Miss Kaylee was in. She decided to go up to the third floor on her own.

When Miss Jillian had given her a tour of the house the first day she was there, she had opened the door to the old attic so Bonnie could see what was behind the door and had warned her not to go in there. For one thing, it was very dusty, and Bonnie didn't really like to get dirty. But this was an emergency, so she decided to look in the attic for the books next, even if it was messy. The door creaked when she opened it, and she looked around to make sure no one came out to see what the noise was. She stepped in and pulled the door closed behind her.

It was midafternoon, so the sun was still quite bright outside and provided enough light through the dormer windows that she could see. Still, the room was gloomy and a little scary. She picked her way carefully through the piles of stuff in the attic, trying not to touch anything except when she had to, to see if the books were hidden beneath or behind something.

Ahead she saw a tall piece of wooden furniture with two doors that met in the middle. It reminded her of a story her mother had read to her about a little girl and her two brothers and sister who passed through something called a wardrobe into a magical world where animals could talk like people. The story had made her long to have brothers and sisters too, even though it seemed like they didn't always get along. She teared up. "If I had a brother or a sister, I wouldn't be all alone in this big old house now."

She sniffled and wiped her tears on the back of her hand before opening one of the doors on the tall piece of furniture. She was disappointed that there were no fur coats hanging there like in the story, but she decided to investigate. She thought if someone wanted to hide the books, this would be the perfect spot. It was dark inside, so she stepped in and set Mr. Benj'min at her feet. She bent over and ran one hand along a back corner. Before she realized what was happening, the door closed behind her with a click.

She felt for the latch, but there was nothing inside that she could find to open the door. She pushed and pounded on both doors, and yelled and cried for help, but no one came. She finally gave up and lay down, sobbing until she fell into an exhausted sleep.

13

Jillian was able to carry Florence's luggage down to the foyer in one trip. She placed it all next to the front door and then went into her office to stash the yellow booklet she had reclaimed from Florence's suitcase. She planned to do some research on her computer later to see if she could find out something about it. She had no intention of mentioning it to Mr. Oglethorpe. What could Florence say about it anyway? "Where's that book I was trying to steal?"

Jillian headed for the kitchen to make a cup of tea. She put the water on to boil and opened the cabinet to survey its contents in order to decide which of many possibilities it would be today. She grabbed a tin, which displayed a unicorn serving tea to a lion that was wearing a crown, plus the words *Queen's Blend Tea* on the side. It looked like something Aunt Cornelia had ordered online. In her best British accent, which wasn't all that good, she said, "I think we shall have the Queen's tea today."

She plunked a couple of teaspoons of the loose-leaf tea in the bottom of a teapot and put the kettle on. She was reaching for a teacup and saucer from the cabinet when the back door opened, and Bertie and Cornelia walked in.

Cornelia looked around. "Where's Bonnie?"

Jillian smiled. That was the question she usually asked Cornelia these days. They were all getting used to having the little girl around. They would miss her when her mother finally came to pick her up. "She's taking a nap upstairs. How was the meeting?"

Bertie sighed. "It was okay. Annalise made a gluten-free

cake for us to try. Needless to say, that's one recipe that's going back to the drawing board. I think that might be the first time we've ever had something that didn't get eaten up during the meeting."

"It was probably just a bad recipe," said Cornelia. "I've heard that gluten-free baked goods can be very tasty."

Bertie rolled her eyes. "I'll believe that when I taste it, which hasn't happened yet."

Jillian decided this conversation was bound to go nowhere, so she changed the subject to the call she'd received from Charles Oglethorpe. She was just about to tell them the part where she found the yellow booklet in Florence's suitcase when the doorbell rang. She stole a glance at the kitchen clock on the wall. "That must be him now." She called over her shoulder as she headed to answer it, "Would you pour the water in the teapot when it boils?"

She glanced into the library as she walked past. Houston and Chester had made themselves comfortable in a couple of old leather armchairs. Chester was reading a thick book, its faded dust jacket discarded on the table next to him. Houston was slouched down with his brown fedora covering his eyes, and his snores could be heard in the foyer. She continued on past.

The bell rang again just before she reached the door. She opened it to a sour-looking man in a rumpled suit. She tried to remember that he'd had to drive across the state to come to his wife's side after she'd been poisoned, and he had every right to look unhappy and unkempt. But something told her that he was not a pleasant person in the best of situations.

"Is this everything?" he demanded, his tone brusque.

"It's everything she came with, as far as I can tell," she replied, matching his tone. She softened it a bit. "How is Florence? I hope she can leave the hospital soon."

His tone softened as well. "They say they'll release her tomorrow morning."

"I'm relieved to hear that, Mr. Oglethorpe. Please give her our best wishes for a speedy recovery."

He looked like he was about to say something nice in return, but then the sour look returned to his features, and he said only, "We'll be by tomorrow to pick up Florence's car." He collected the luggage and was off without another word.

She closed the door and turned away. Hearing footsteps on the stairs, Jillian looked up to see Kaylee bouncing down the steps. "I was just making some tea in the kitchen. Would you care for a cup?" Jillian offered.

"That sounds like a fine idea. I don't suppose you have any of your bakery treats to go with it?"

"Surely we can scrounge up something."

When they walked into the kitchen, Cornelia and Bertie had already launched into preparing what Jillian was sure would end up being a high tea that even the Queen would approve. Another kettle of water was on to boil, and Cornelia was pulling a variety of things from the refrigerator, including thin-sliced meats and jams while Bertie mixed up a big batch of what looked like scone dough, based on its thick and sticky consistency.

Bertie looked up at them. "Why don't you girls pitch in? We decided we should make enough for everyone."

"I should have thought of that," said Jillian.

"Yes, you should have," said Bertie. She said it matter-of-factly, without any trace of censure, but the words were still sharp.

Jillian sighed inwardly. She was used to Bertie's terse manner, but sometimes it still caught her wrong. She shook it off.

"When we're almost finished here," said Bertie to Jillian, "you can run and get the others to join us in the living room. We've already invited Burton to join us after he's done setting the traps. We saw him on the way in."

"What traps?" asked Jillian. She looked at Cornelia, who didn't seem the least bit surprised by Bertie's comment.

"For the raccoons. I called Burton this morning before we left for church and asked if he'd bring over his raccoon traps this afternoon. I remembered him telling me about a problem he had with them a few years back, and he said he'd be glad to do it." Bertie spared a glance at Cornelia while she divided the dough in two and briskly patted each half into a thick circle.

"They aren't like bear traps are they?" asked Jillian. "I don't want them hurt."

"I'm sure they're just cages," Kaylee said. "That's the typical method for capturing raccoons. You can bait them with cat food. You'll want to make sure that Possum stays indoors until they're captured. Jumbo marshmallows actually work really well too. They're round and white so they look like eggs. And raccoons love the sweetness."

Jillian looked at Kaylee with surprise. "How do you know so much about it?"

"Oh, being a veterinary nurse, you learn about all sorts of animals. Raccoons are especially worrisome to pet owners because they can carry disease, not the least of which is rabies."

Now Kaylee's lack of action after Florence's collapse made sense. Her specialty was animals, not people.

Cornelia harrumphed. She no doubt considered the lack of a ghostly reason behind the events to be a loss. "I still don't see how raccoons could be responsible for the things that happened in the barn—the door wide open, for example."

"It's just a dead bolt, right?" said Kaylee. "That's child's play for a raccoon. They're smart, and they remember what they figure out. But that was probably just going out from the inside. I'd imagine they have another way in. They can enter through crawl spaces, air ducts, chimneys, you name it. If there's a way, they'll find it."

"Well, I hope Burton's traps work," said Jillian. "What will he do with them after they're captured?"

"Well, to tell you the truth, they're often put down," said Kaylee. "But you might be able to find a wildlife rehabilitator that would allow him to release them on their land, as long as it's at least five miles from here. Any closer and they'd just return."

"Where can I find a wildlife rehabilitator?" asked Jillian.

"You'll have to look online. And you will most likely have to pay a fee. They'll need to be tested for disease before they're released."

"Great." Jillian began to think Gooder's offer to shoot them might have been easier. But then she thought of their cute, masked faces and knew she'd cough up the money if it meant they could be saved.

The conversation moved on to other things, including speculation as to whether Patricia would be spending the night in jail. A short time later, when the tea was nearly ready, their conversation was interrupted by Burton knocking on the back door, then stepping inside. "Hello, ladies. I'll just wash up and be with you in a moment."

"We're set up in the living room, Burton," Bertie called after him. "Jillian, you run this tray into the living room and then go and get the others."

She found Waldon and Avery already in the living room talking with Victor when she carried in the tray of snacks. After that was done, she stuck her head in the library to tell Chester and Houston. Both men were on their feet at once, indicating they were hungry. That left Dorothea. Patricia had not yet returned from the police station, if she was going to be able to come back to Belle Haven at all. Jillian hoped she would be released. She didn't believe for a moment that Patricia was responsible for the poisoning. In fact, it was increasingly hard for her to believe that any of her guests had done it.

Jillian went up the stairs and knocked on Dorothea's door. Dorothea answered, looking as if she could use some cheering up. While Dorothea went down the stairs, Jillian went to wake Bonnie.

She opened the door slowly and peeked inside. She was surprised to see the bed empty. She opened the door wide and stepped inside. "Bonnie?" She thought maybe the little girl had heard her coming and might be hiding, so she looked around the room—behind the curtains, under the bed, in the closet. She stood in the middle of the room, thinking. *She's probably downstairs playing with the dollhouse or coloring.*

Returning to the living room, Jillian found that the guests had already begun to dig into the tea and snacks. The absence of Florence, and the police having taken Patricia for questioning seemed to have eased the tension among her guests. Jillian looked behind the sofa to see if Bonnie was there, and when the child was not, she casually asked if anyone had seen her. When they answered in the negative, she started to make a search of the entire downstairs.

She stepped in the kitchen. Bertie was there. "Have you seen Bonnie?"

"Not since church. Isn't she in your room?"

"No, and I can't find her." She looked at Bertie with worried eyes, panic rising in her throat like bile.

"Did anything happen?" asked Bertie.

"What do you mean?"

"Anything that would make her want to hide or . . . run away?"

Jillian shook her head slowly, but then remembered her momentary harshness with the girl. "I might have said a couple of harsh words without thinking, but I apologized. I thought it was fine." She thought of the little girl's hurt expression, and the way she had pulled away from her after that. Her eyes widened. "You don't think she'd run off, do you?"

Bertie dried her hands on a dish towel. "I hope not."

Jillian went back to the living room and asked the guests again if they had seen Bonnie that afternoon. When everyone said they hadn't, they all got involved in the search, each guest checking his or her own room. Beside herself, Jillian practically flew from room to room, barely looking as she did so. Her worst fear was that Bonnie might have left the house, and the thought of her lost out there somewhere clouded Jillian's judgment. She checked the third floor, except for Waldon's room, even opening the door to the attic and calling Bonnie's name, though she didn't think she would be there. She closed the door quickly and headed back downstairs. With no sign of Bonnie in the house, Burton, Houston, Chester, and Kaylee were preparing to expand the search to outdoors.

In the midst of this hubbub, the front door opened, and Laura Lee walked in with Patricia, who looked exhausted. Jillian was standing in the door of her office, about to dial 911 to get the police involved in looking for Bonnie. The sight of Laura Lee in her uniform flooded her with relief. After Jillian explained the situation in a rushed manner, Laura Lee took over, speaking calmly. She first suggested searching the house again systematically, starting at the top floor and working their way down. If Bonnie wasn't found, she'd call in backup.

Laura Lee accompanied Jillian back up to the third floor. Jillian spoke much more quickly and in a higher pitch than was normal for her. "I already checked up here, and Waldon checked his room. What if she went outside? It'll be dark in just a few hours."

"Jillian, I know this is stressful, but you've got to calm down.

We'll do a thorough search of the house, and then, if need be, we'll expand from there. We'll find her, but we have to be smart about it. Okay?"

Jillian forced herself to take a deep breath at her friend's soothing words. "Okay."

They started in Waldon's room and proceeded through the other rooms until they got to the attic door.

"I don't think she's in there," said Jillian. "I warned her not to go in there when she first came."

"We'll check to be sure," Laura Lee replied patiently. "Kids don't always listen to warnings."

That was true. Why hadn't Jillian considered that before?

Laura Lee opened the door. With the sun lower in the sky, it was hard to see. "Is there a light switch?"

"On your left."

She flipped the switch, stepped inside, and called Bonnie's name loudly. They both heard a child's wail.

The rest of the day was a blur. Jillian didn't ever recall such a range of emotions as when she opened the door of the armoire to find Bonnie, her eyes red and her face flushed and streaked with tears. But she was safe. Jillian's feelings went beyond simple relief. Bonnie wrapped her arms around Jillian's neck and wouldn't let go, and Jillian didn't want her to.

It was obvious that the little girl had forgiven Jillian.

After things had settled down and Laura Lee had left Belle Haven, Jillian ran a bubble bath for Bonnie. She sat by the tub as Bonnie told her what had happened.

The little girl suddenly stopped mid-story. "Oh, Miss Jillian. I forgot Mr. Benj'min. He's still up there."

"Not to worry. I'll run up and get him later."

"Will he be all right?"

"He'll be fine."

It was bedtime when she and Bonnie remembered the stuffed bunny. Jillian tucked Bonnie in and told her she would be right back with Mr. Benjamin. She went up the stairs and opened the creaky door to the attic. It was a cloudy night, so the inside of the attic was a sooty black with no moonlight from outside to take off the edge. Jillian switched on the light, which helped, but gave the room an oppressive feel as if the darkness didn't appreciate her intrusion. She shivered, imagining what it might have been like for Bonnie if she hadn't been found and had spent the night in there. She made her way to the armoire, telling herself that at the first chance, she was going to remove that latch.

She wished she'd brought a flashlight. Nevertheless, she found Mr. Benjamin easily by feel. He wasn't lying flat on the floor of the armoire, but was leaning against something. After she picked him up, her curiosity got the better of her. She felt around and discovered it was a stack of books. *More books?* she thought. She picked up the top one. It was *The Story of the Treasure Seekers*, one of the books she had found in the crate in the attic. She took out the rest of the books one by one. All the missing children's books were there. She balanced the stack of books on one arm and tucked the bunny under the other. She decided she'd hide the books herself this time, somewhere in her own room, perhaps in the bottom of the trunk where extra quilts were stored.

As she headed back down the steps to the second floor, she pictured each of her guests. They had all been so helpful in looking for Bonnie. She didn't want to think that any one of them was the culprit, but she reminded herself that one of them had switched the labels on Dorothea's spices, and someone must have poisoned the sherry. She knew that Florence had tried to steal the yellow booklet. And now, one of her guests had taken the books and placed them in the armoire. And how had Bonnie gotten locked into it? How many in this group were dishonest? Two or three? All of them?

Any way she looked at it, it was growing harder and harder to believe she could trust any of them.

Early the next morning, Jillian was at her computer before she even got a cup of coffee, trying to find out something about the yellow booklet, but the searches she had tried so far yielded very little. There was a scholarly article about the use of steam power in British gristmills in the eighteenth century. Brooke Flour Mill was among those mentioned, but there was no other information given. It didn't appear that it even existed anymore. She gave up, grabbed the booklet, and went to the kitchen to talk to Bertie.

Bertie was sitting at the breakfast table, eating a bowl of oatmeal and reading the morning newspaper, which was spread open across the table.

Jillian dropped the yellow booklet in the middle of the paper and sat down heavily. "I didn't get a chance to tell you yesterday, but I found this in Florence's suitcase. It was in that crate I found in the attic. Can you think of any reason she'd try to steal it?"

Bertie looked at Jillian over her reading glasses with some annoyance, but she picked up the booklet. "And a good morning to you too," she said with a fair amount of sarcasm. She flipped through the booklet. "I don't know. Maybe she just wanted to see if the recipes were any good. Could be that she was going to ask to borrow it, but with all that happened—" Bertie stopped, her expression becoming puzzled. She turned a few more pages without saying a word. Then she got up from her chair and walked to the built-in bookcase in the kitchen. Bertie grabbed the first edition of *Blissful Baking*, Patricia Smith's best-selling cookbook.

Jillian watched as Bertie opened the cookbook and began comparing it side by side with the small booklet. After flipping through several pages, Bertie looked up at Jillian. "I think I know why Florence wanted this. The recipes are exactly the same. The cookbook has been Americanized in spelling and units of measurement, and it's been filled out with photographs and helpful hints, but the recipes are basically lifted straight from this booklet."

Jillian gasped. Patricia Smith was a fraud?

She thought of the confrontation between Patricia and Florence in the library. Patricia had definitely been angry, and Florence was . . . smug? She remembered Florence's boast about publishing a new cookbook and going national with her TV show. Had she used the booklet to try to blackmail Patricia?

"This must have been the secret that Florence was referring to in her statement," Jillian said. "Did Patricia say anything to you last evening about her interview with the police?"

"No, she was pretty quiet," Bertie replied. "And then after Bonnie was found, things seemed to get awkward again. Victor was the only one who really talked to her. She went up to her room right after supper."

"Patricia told us she was desperate to earn a living after her husband died. If we're assuming that everything that came out of that crate was printed before the date on the newspaper—1928—would there be any danger of copyright infringement? I don't even know if something like that would have been legally protected."

"Maybe not, but what would it do to Patricia's reputation? Even the other things she's published and her TV show would all be questioned. People would wonder whether anything she's done is authentic. And it would depend on how important it was to Patricia at this stage in her life."

"Pretty important, I think," said Jillian. "She's old enough that she could have retired after her show was canceled, but instead she branched out into producing this new show. That doesn't sound like someone who wanted to just rest on her laurels."

"But is a secret like this enough of a reason to try to kill someone?" Bertie shook her head. "I know we've only just met her, but I just can't see Patricia doing something like that."

"I know. I don't want to believe it either. But someone put that poison in the bottle." Jillian rubbed her forehead. "We don't even know for sure if Florence was the intended victim."

They were interrupted by a knock on the back door. It was Gooder, whose habit had been to report each morning. Jillian was sure it was for the breakfast he had come to expect. She had asked him to continue with the job as long as the show's equipment was there, which she hoped wouldn't be much longer.

Jillian picked up the booklet. "I'm going to stash this in my office. Let's keep it to ourselves until we know more. I want to talk to Patricia directly." She looked toward the door. "I guess I'll have to feed Gooder this morning."

Bertie stood up. "No, you go on. I'll take care of it."

"Don't you have to get to work?"

"I decided to keep the bakery closed today since Lenora's family is in town and we've got all this going on. I posted it on the door on Saturday."

"I can't deny I'm glad you'll be around. I just pray this day turns out to be less stressful. Did Laura Lee give you any indication how long we're going to have to house these people?"

"No. But I wouldn't count on them leaving anytime soon."

Jillian tried to do little things that morning to try to bring some semblance of order to her thoughts. She confirmed with Avery that she still had *Mrs. Beeton's Book of Household Management* in her room. At least no one had tried to steal that so far.

She called Burton to let him know that Gooder had confirmed the capture of the raccoons.

"Great," Burton told her. "I know a place that will take them. I'll swing by later this morning to pick them up."

Jillian thanked him and hung up, then looked for Patricia, hoping to speak to her alone. Unfortunately, she found that right after breakfast Patricia, Houston, and Victor had closed themselves off in the library.

Jillian worked in her office at her computer while Bonnie sat coloring on a soft blanket on the horsehair sofa. Since Bonnie had been found in the attic, Jillian's protective instincts had jumped off the chart. They'd had a call from Lilith that morning to let them know that her flight was scheduled to arrive in Atlanta late on Tuesday. Her mother, Margaret, now returned from her vacation, was going to pick her up at the airport, and she would be at Belle Haven to pick up Bonnie on Wednesday. *Only two more days.* Jillian was torn. She wanted Bonnie to be safe with her mother again, but her heart ached at the thought of letting her go, especially to the far side of the country.

Occasionally Jillian could hear the sounds of voices filtering into the large foyer from the discussion in the library, Houston's in particular, but the solid wooden doors of Belle Haven tended to mute the details unless one could stand right next to it with a glass to the door and one's ear at the other end of the glass. Not that Jillian had ever tried that. Or that Bertie had ever caught her.

After about an hour, Victor emerged and asked Bertie to join them. A short time later all four emerged from the library and went throughout the house until they had found everyone, including Jillian and Cornelia, and had asked them to attend a meeting in the living room. By the time they had gathered, Bonnie was occupied with the dollhouse. Jillian sat close by to keep an eye on her.

When everyone was settled, Patricia took the floor. "We want to try to salvage this episode as much as we possibly can. The crew is still in town, and we're not scheduled to arrive at our next venue until Wednesday. That's in Tennessee and not that far from here, and we may be able to put that off a day if it helps us get what we need for this episode. I have reason to believe the police will have answers today. We've already taken some footage around Moss Hollow to use as filler as we need it. And, fortunately, we do have one day of baking filmed, but we can't continue with the contest portion of the show until—"

"What show is there without the contest?" Avery interrupted.

"There are a few other things we can do to fill in, and I hope that we'll be cleared to continue with the contest before—"

"Do you know something about their investigation that you're not telling us?" Chester demanded. "Why did they pick you up for questioning yesterday? I think we have the right to know."

"I agree," said Patricia, "and I'll get to that, but first, I want to tell you that one of our hosts at Belle Haven, Mrs. Bertie Harper, has agreed to serve as a judge in Florence's place. Bertie is an expert baker who has run a successful bakery for decades, so she is well qualified. This morning, we'll need to redo the interviews where Florence asked about your recipes and some other things, but Houston will work that out. Then, this afternoon, we'd like you contestants to serve as an audience at The Chocolate Shoppe Bakery while Victor interviews Mrs. Harper about her life as a professional baker. I think our viewers will find that very interesting."

"What about Florence?" asked Waldon.

Patricia's eyebrows arched. "It's unfortunate what happened

to her. I wish her a speedy recovery, but she will not be returning as judge for this episode in any case."

If not for the situation, Jillian was pretty sure the contestants would have applauded. As it was, there was an awkward silence. What with yesterday's events, Jillian had forgotten to tell anyone else that Florence was to be released from the hospital that morning. She opened her mouth to relay the information when the front doorbell rang followed by a persistent pounding on the door.

Jillian jumped up from her chair and practically ran to open the door. Florence, followed closely by her husband, stormed through the doorway without waiting for an invitation to enter. Jillian just barely had time to marvel at the negative energy that washed over her as the couple took a stand in the middle of the foyer. *Maybe I do have a touch of Aunt Cornelia's "spirit sense" after all.*

As soon as Charles laid eyes on Jillian he shook his finger at her. "I warned you. I said if anything was missing from my wife's luggage, we wouldn't stand for it."

"What exactly is missing?" asked Jillian. She tried to keep her face as passive as possible while she wondered at the audacity of this couple. She knew exactly what was missing, and it was safely tucked away in her desk drawer at that moment.

Florence's eyes narrowed. "I don't have to tell you anything. I demand to search my room and any other part of this house I need to until I find it. Someone was in my luggage, and I'm not leaving here until I have satisfaction."

"Excuse me, but without some sort of idea what's missing, I can't help you."

"Are you denying us access?"

"As I said, if you tell me what's missing, I will check to see if I can find it. You are no longer a guest here, so I'm within my rights."

Florence sputtered. "I'll call the police!"

Jillian was ready to call her bluff. "Go ahead. They'll ask you the same question."

Florence paused for a moment, then landed on a new line. "Where's Patricia? I want to speak to her."

Jillian hesitated. The last thing she wanted was to have this play out in front of everyone in the house. She was about to suggest they go to the library to talk when Patricia entered the foyer.

Florence practically crowed. "There you are! I can't believe the police let you go. If you want to stay out of jail, you'll do just what I tell you, or I'll let everyone know what you really are—a fraud."

Patricia's voice was cold as steel. "I've already informed the police of your attempt to blackmail me. I was telling Houston and Victor about it when you were . . . taken ill, and they will confirm everything. I will tell you what I told the police. I did not poison you. I was about to fire you, so consider this your notice. You are fired."

"You can't do that! I have a contract."

"And the conditions of your termination will be met. But you will not be appearing on this program now or in any future production that I am associated with."

"When I'm done with you, there won't be any future productions," Florence said with a sneer.

Patricia kept her cool. "Time will tell. In the meantime, you might be wise to concentrate on explaining your behavior to the police. Blackmail is considered theft by extortion in Georgia, carrying a sentence of up to ten years."

Florence looked at her in disbelief. "I'm the victim here! How dare you threaten me?"

"I'm not threatening you, Florence. I'm trying to help you understand how serious this is. You are not going to get your way by trying to steamroll me. It won't work. I suggest you take this as a life lesson and head home to Atlanta—if the police will clear you to leave the area, which may be doubtful."

"You can't speak to my wife like that," blustered Charles. "You will both be hearing from our lawyer."

Neither Patricia nor Jillian answered.

"Let's go, Charlie," said Florence. As she turned to leave, she added, "You haven't heard the last of me!"

Jillian hoped it was another bluff. They left without a mention of "their" missing property. She sincerely hoped to never set eyes on either of them again, on- or offscreen.

Now if only she could survive the rest of her guests' stay.

When Jillian and Patricia returned to the living room, people were returning to their seats in stunned silence, having gathered near the door to find out what was being said in the foyer. But the silence didn't last long. Houston took over and started getting things moving. Questions were set aside for the moment, and production seemed to be back on track even though there was still the problem of who had put cyanide in Avery's bottle of sherry. Jillian guessed everyone would be safe as long as there was no taste testing to be done, but what would happen if and when the police figured out who the culprit was? She guessed that bridge would be crossed when they came to it.

The contestants went up to their rooms to retrieve their totes. Chester, Kaylee, and Dorothea reappeared and headed on out to the hall. Jillian suspected that Avery was changing her outfit since they would be on camera today. Waldon—she wasn't sure about him. He was such an odd duck, she felt like she had come to know him least of all. She thought about asking him if he wanted to move down to Florence's former room on the second floor, but she really hoped that they wouldn't be there long enough to make that change necessary.

Jillian had been surprised that Bertie would agree to be a judge on the show, but it did seem to be the perfect solution, and it certainly wouldn't hurt The Chocolate Shoppe's profile.

It was a good solution unless all did not go as smoothly as Patricia hoped and there was another "incident." Suddenly Jillian wasn't sure it was such a good idea.

She went to the kitchen talk to Cornelia about the food

situation. "Since we weren't expecting to still have company today, do I need to run to the store?"

"Yes please. I've already started a list. And I called Maudie and Wanda Jean to see if they could come over to help again. Of course they were glad to."

Jillian just stopped herself from groaning. She did appreciate their willingness to pitch in. She just wished that they were a little less free to the general public with the details of what was going on at Belle Haven. "Don't mention anything to them about what happened with Florence, will you?"

Cornelia tilted her head. "I don't see why it would come up."

"Of course it will come up, Aunt Cornelia. Please, let's just try to keep this within the confines of Belle Haven. At least for now."

"I'll do my best. But you know, Jillian, secrets have a way of festering and making situations worse."

"And gossip has a tendency to distort the truth."

"Point taken," said Cornelia. She wrote a couple more things on the list, tore off the sheet and handed it to Jillian. "Are you taking Bonnie with you?"

"Yes. I just have to run up to my bedroom to grab my purse."

She walked to the living room first where Bonnie was seated at the small table, studying the horse and carriage that Savannah had cleaned so carefully.

"Do you want to go to town with me?"

Not answering the question, Bonnie looked up. "Have you ever ridden in a carriage, Miss Jillian?"

"Yes I have. It didn't look exactly like that one though."

"Was it fun?"

"Yes it was fun. I would even call it exhilarating."

"What's ex'il'rating mean?"

Jillian took a deep breath. She should have known that question was coming. "It means something that makes you feel especially happy or excited."

"When I see Mama again, I will be ex'il'rating."

Jillian bent over and kissed Bonnie on the forehead. She didn't bother about the pronunciation or the usage. "I know you will, sweetheart. It's only a couple more days. I know that doesn't seem like it's soon enough, but it will go quickly."

Bonnie looked like she was going to cry. "But then I'll miss you."

Jillian felt her own eyes well up. She took Bonnie's hand and led her over to the sofa where she lifted the child onto her lap. "I'm going to miss you too. But we'll see each other again. You'll be back in Georgia to visit your grandparents and your grandmamma Genevieve, and you are always welcome at Belle Haven."

Even as she said those words, Jillian couldn't help but think of the day she left for college in California. It had been twenty years before she stepped foot in Moss Hollow again. How had she let that happen? She knew the answer. There was always something else—first it was schoolwork or the travel expense, and then later it was her career or it was her former fiancé . . . She stopped there and looked at Bonnie's face, trying to imagine it as it might look in twenty years' time. The little girl had captured Jillian's heart in just a few days. She couldn't imagine going twenty years without seeing her.

"Will you come visit me in Wash'ton state?" Bonnie's eyes pleaded.

"You know what? I would love to do that, and I'm going to. I promise," she said, meaning it with all her heart. "And maybe I will ask your mama if you could stay here a week during the summer each year. Would you like that?"

Bonnie beamed. "Yes."

That settled, Bonnie got down from Jillian's lap and Jillian stood up. "Now, about going to town. Are you with me?"

"Yes, Miss Jillian."

"I have to go upstairs to get my purse."

Bonnie took her hand. "I'll come too." They walked only a few steps before Bonnie spoke again. "If I get a baby brother or baby sister, can I bring them to Belle Haven in the summer too?"

Jillian laughed. "Only if you teach them to be as good as you are."

It wasn't until after the lunch cleanup was taken care of and all the guests, plus Bertie, had gone to The Chocolate Shoppe to film Bertie's interview that Jillian had a chance to run her purse back upstairs. Cornelia was with Bonnie in the living room, attempting to teach her how to finger-crochet a simple chain with thick, blue yarn, telling her she could make friendship bracelets to give to the new friends she would make when she lived in Washington.

When Jillian entered her bedroom, an out-of-place, but not unpleasant, odor met her nostrils. It seemed an odd combination to her—woodsy and masculine, but with a hint of something feminine like vanilla. Someone had been in her room. She looked around to see if anything was missing. Nothing seemed disturbed.

She opened the closet and several drawers, but everything seemed to be where it normally was. It was her habit to leave her purse hanging on one of the hooks on a wall shelf, where there also was hanging a sweater and a couple of scarves, but now she wondered if she should hide it somewhere. Even with all that had happened, she hadn't been locking her bedroom door, but now she thought she might have to. She looked around for hiding places, and her gaze fell on the old trunk where she had placed the children's books beneath the multiple quilts that were stored there.

With a sinking feeling, she lifted the lid and started carefully unpacking the quilts one by one until she lifted the bottom one. It was as she feared. The books were gone. She looked around the room again. How careful someone had been. They'd even left *A Little Princess* on her nightstand. If she hadn't noticed the scent, she doubted she would've even thought to check to see if the books remained in their hiding place.

She put the quilts back in the trunk, closed the lid, and then hid her purse in the bottom of the closet, thinking all the time that it wasn't a very good hiding place, but she couldn't think of a better one. She removed the antique brass key from the keyhole of the bedroom door so she could lock the door when she left. Her hand was on the crystal doorknob when her phone rang. She grabbed it from her pocket and looked at the screen, hoping it was Savannah. She needed to talk this out.

It was Hunter.

"I was wondering if you and Bonnie would care to join me this evening. I thought we could go over to the fairgrounds for the county fair's Bluegrass & Barbecue Bash. I intended to call you this morning, but a call came into the coroner's office and I had to run over to—well, never mind about that. I just got back home."

"Oh, Hunter, that would be really nice, but I don't think I can." Her voice betrayed her disquiet that someone who didn't belong there had been in her room and had taken the books.

He picked up on it. "What's wrong?"

She sighed. "Nothing."

He was silent, waiting.

She gave it up. "Okay, everything." She walked over and sat on the edge of the bed, and the words poured out. "You know how it is when you think everything will go like clockwork, and then everything goes wrong? First it was the raccoons, but Aunt

Cornelia thought it was a ghost, and I had to pay Gooder to be a night watchman—which hurts our bottom line—and he's going to be out there until the equipment is removed—which I'm starting to think will never happen—and then Florence was trying to blackmail Patricia, but I didn't know it until after I found the yellow booklet in Florence's luggage and Bertie said it was just like *Blissful Baking*, but then, before that, Florence got poisoned and blamed Patricia, but Patricia says she didn't do it, and then Bonnie got trapped in the armoire in the attic, and I found the books that had been missing, but now the books are gone again, and I don't know who is behind all this or why they're doing it, and I don't know how long these people will have to stay here, and I don't trust any of them, but I want to because I like most of them, and I don't know what to do."

There was silence on the line.

"Hunter? Are you there?"

"I'm here, Jillian. I'm . . . processing."

"You probably think I'm crazy."

"No I don't. It's just a lot to take in. I think I'm missing some details. Would it help if I came over so we could talk face to face? I could run over to the fairgrounds and pick up some barbecue to go—enough for all your guests. How many do you have?"

"There are eight guests now. They'd probably actually enjoy going to the bash, but they aren't supposed to leave the environs of Moss Hollow. Since the fairgrounds are located close to Painter's Ridge, it's out of reach."

"Why can't they leave?"

"They're all under suspicion for the poisoning of Florence."

"And who is Florence?"

Jillian realized with some surprise that Hunter was probably not on Maudie and Wanda Jean's list of people to tell the latest news. These days she assumed that everyone in Moss Hollow knew her business. "Florence was one of the judges for the TV show they're filming here. Now Florence is gone, and Bertie has taken the job."

"But Florence couldn't have died, or I would have been called in."

"No, she's all right now. They released her from the hospital this morning. Patricia fired her."

There was a slight pause. "Why don't I call Sheriff Henderson and see if I can get your group released to go to the bash for the evening instead?"

"Could you do that?"

"I can certainly try. I'll call you back shortly."

The screen showed that Hunter had ended the call. Jillian sat there a minute. The thought of having a night out sounded wonderful. She could forget everything and just listen to bluegrass music, maybe dance a little, and eat from the wide variety of Southern-style barbecues that were always offered at the bash. An evening of bluegrass and barbecue sounded like heaven.

Hopefully it would be as good as it sounded.

16

Jillian was slightly surprised when Hunter called back and said they could all go to the fairgrounds for the evening. She was even more surprised when everyone, even Bertie, was enthusiastic about going. When Hunter arrived around five, he had a stern talk with them about the terms of the outing and told them that the sheriff would be at Belle Haven early the next morning to talk to them, but declined to give details.

They carpooled in the bakery van, which Bertie drove, and the production van, driven by Houston. Jillian and Bonnie rode with Hunter in his car. As they neared their destination, Jillian could hear the lively sounds of banjos, guitars, mandolins, harmonicas, fiddles, and bass fiddles, and the smell of smoke and barbecued meat drifted pleasantly through the car's open windows as they slowed to join the line of cars entering the fairgrounds.

The parking was well organized by men directing the cars to line up in the grassy parking area, so it didn't take long. It was a bit of a walk to the area around the outdoor stage where the musicians were playing, but there were still open areas to be found among the crowd of people, and they set up the lawn chairs and laid out the blankets that they had brought along to sit on.

Bonnie was understandably excited, and Jillian was pleased when she found children nearby to dance and play with. Jillian had wanted to get her to eat something, but gave up the fourth time the girl looked longingly toward the other children. Jillian figured the child wasn't about to starve and would eat when she was hungry, so she let her go have fun.

They stayed until about nine thirty. The bash was scheduled

to end at eleven, but Cornelia, Bertie, and Patricia especially were tired.

Belle Haven seemed quiet and still when they walked inside after the noise and activity at the fairgrounds. They kept their voices low as they made their way to their rooms. Jillian thought that perhaps knowing that Sheriff Henderson would be there in the morning was causing some concern—at least to the guilty party or parties. Still, the bash had been a nice break from reality.

Bonnie was almost asleep before her head hit the pillow. Jillian was fine with that. She didn't think she could keep her eyes open to read more chapters anyway.

Jillian woke hours later with a raging thirst. *It was that salt-rub beef barbecue I sampled.* She was reaching for the carafe she kept by the bed when she remembered it was empty. She had intended to take it downstairs to wash and refill it, but had been interrupted before she got the job done. Bonnie was sound asleep, so Jillian got up and put on her bathrobe to go downstairs for a drink of water.

As it was another cloudy night, the overhead dome didn't provide much in the way of light, and her flashlight was a necessity for making it down the steps and to the kitchen. Once her mission was accomplished, she was in the foyer on her way back to the staircase when she stepped on something that almost made her cry out in pain. She hopped on one foot until she could sit down. She crossed her ankle over her knee and shone the flashlight on the bottom of her foot, then on the floor to find she'd stepped on an earring. *Such a small thing to cause so much hurt.* She rubbed her foot to massage away the sting.

She looked at the earring more closely. She'd seen it before, just that evening. It was one Avery had worn to the bash. Avery had gone to great lengths to explain to everyone that her jewelry that evening was a replica of a set that Princess Diana had worn to some event that Jillian had already forgotten. Jillian had thought it was overkill for a bluegrass event, but it didn't really matter. She thought Avery, and all the rest of the guests, had enjoyed the outing, and they had needed something like that as much as she had. Wardrobe was a minor thing.

As she examined the earring, she noticed that the backing was missing. It was probably on the floor somewhere, but she'd look for it tomorrow. She rubbed her foot again, got up, and made her way up the steps. In the second-floor hallway, she noticed something she hadn't on her way downstairs—that there was light shining from beneath and around the edge of Avery's bedroom door, as if it was slightly ajar. Curious, she tiptoed to the door and found that it was not latched. "Avery?" she asked softly and pushed the door, which slowly swung open.

Avery's bed had been slept in, but Avery wasn't in it. Jillian walked in and placed the earring on the dresser. There was no sign of any of her luggage. Jillian looked in the closet. There was nothing of Avery's there either. She was gone.

Jillian sat on the bed and tried to think what to do. She had thought of Avery as a likely victim, but never as the perpetrator. She must have decided to leave in case Sheriff Henderson was coming to arrest her.

Jillian thought of her options. If she called 911, the whole place would be in an uproar. She pictured flashing lights, blazing sirens, and police officers swarming over Belle Haven. She could just imagine the *Moss Hollow Chronicle*'s next headline: *Belle Family at the Center of Criminal Activity*. That last might be a stretch, but by the time the town gossip mill got hold of it, it would likely be as good—or rather, as bad—as that.

Gooder was out at the barn for what she hoped was the last night. She could go out and tell him. But the thought of making another middle-of-the-night trek out there in her nightgown and rubber boots was out of the question. She'd embarrassed herself enough on that front. Besides, there was the fact that he had shot off a couple of rounds in the middle of the night just to scare off some raccoons. What chaos might ensue if she told him about this? She imagined him waking up the entire household, not with gunshots, but with accusations.

She knew that calling 911 or talking to Gooder might be the logical thing to do, but then Hunter's face floated into her mind's eye. Hunter, the discreet mortician and coroner, now had at least some understanding of what had been going on at Belle Haven. She'd seek his advice first.

She got up and tiptoed into her bedroom. She laid the flashlight on the dresser and used its light to change into a pair of jeans, a T-shirt, and a light cardigan with three-quarter sleeves. She ran a brush through her hair and gathered it into a ponytail before grabbing the flashlight and then her phone from the nightstand. The glowing clock numbers showed it was nearly four o'clock. She was about to leave the room when she remembered she might need shoes. She flashed the light in the bottom of the closet and grabbed a pair of soft-soled slip-ons. She tucked them under her arm and stepped into the hallway, thankful Bonnie remained asleep.

She went back down the steps and walked into her office, closing the door behind her. She turned on a table lamp before sitting down to put on her shoes and call Hunter. She hesitated with her finger above the screen, but then made the call. He was probably used to being awakened in the middle of the night for police business or for normal business of the mortuary. She sometimes forgot that that was his livelihood, but tonight, a man who was used to being disturbed all hours was just the one she needed.

"Hunter Greyson." His tone was all business. He didn't even sound groggy.

"Hunter, it's Jillian."

"What's wrong?"

"I'm sorry, but I need your advice. Avery's gone."

There was another measured pause. "When you say she's gone, you mean she's left Belle Haven?"

"Well, yes. What did you think I meant?"

"In my line of business, one has to be careful. Can you explain a little more?"

Jillian told him what she had discovered.

"And her car is gone?"

"Oh. I didn't even think to look. I just assumed. Just a sec." She leaned forward to try to see through the windows that were in front of her desk, but with the darkness outside and the moisture that had fogged up the panes, she couldn't see, even after she turned out the light. She went out into the foyer to the front door, opened it, and stepped out onto the front porch, closing the door behind her as quietly as possible, and making sure not to let the screen door slam shut. She scanned the loop where the guests had parked their cars. Avery's SUV was missing.

"Yes. It's gone."

"And only Avery's car is missing?"

Jillian looked again, counting the cars to make sure. "Yes, she drives an SUV, and it's the only one of the guests' vehicles that isn't here."

"I think you're going to have to call the sheriff."

She sighed. "You're right. I'm sorry I bothered you. I guess I was hoping I could wait until later. There could be a reasonable explanation."

"Did you find a note or anything that might say where she's gone?"

Jillian cast her thoughts back to Avery's room. She didn't think there had been a note, but she wasn't sure. "I don't recall seeing one, but after I noticed all her luggage was gone, I didn't really look. I should have thought of that before I called you."

"That's okay. I'm glad that when you needed someone you thought to call me. Didn't you say that Gooder was going to be night watchman again tonight?"

"Yes." She was starting to feel like she had disturbed Hunter for no reason.

"Why don't you first have a look around to see if there's a note from Avery? Then go out and tell him what's happened whether or not you find one. He can decide whether to call the sheriff. That takes the responsibility off you."

"That sounds reasonable." *If only Gooder will be reasonable*, she thought.

"And don't worry. For something like this, at this time of the morning, they aren't going to show up with their lights and sirens going."

"Of course not." She felt rather silly now for thinking that was just what would happen. "Thanks, Hunter."

"Any time, Jillian. If there's anything else I can do, let me know. You can always count on me. I hope you know that."

Jillian smiled. "That's nice to hear. I'll call you back later this morning." She smiled. "*Much* later this morning, to let you know what's going on."

"I'll look forward to hearing your voice again."

She ended the call. She began to think of places she might look for a note from Avery. She'd check the foyer, then Avery's bedroom. She could look in the kitchen on the way out to tell Gooder what she'd found. At least she'd be dressed this time.

Her hand was on the doorknob, ready to head back inside, when she heard a noise behind her. Her head seemed to explode with pain. She saw bright points of light as she felt herself falling forward, and then there was only darkness.

17

J illian woke, having no idea how long she'd been out or where she was. Her head ached so badly that even trying to open her eyes hurt. So she felt, rather than saw, that she was in an enclosed space, lying on a hard surface that was covered with some sort of rough material. Her mouth was gagged with a soft cloth that smelled medicinal and sweet, as if it had been stored with cough drops and mints. Her hands were tied behind her with something that felt rough like the sisal gardening rope Aunt Cornelia had in the garden shed. When she tried to stretch out her legs, she realized that the same rope around her hands was tied around her ankles, making it impossible for her to straighten out.

Eventually she did open her eyes, but she was in total darkness, and even after several minutes, her eyes did not seem to adjust. She closed her eyes again and began to listen. She heard the occasional sound—a thump, a scrape, and other similar sounds, but she couldn't identify them. There were no voices as far as she could tell, but it was as if her ears were swaddled in cotton. Everything sounded muted and far away. She felt herself drifting off again. She tried to resist it, but her head hurt, and she was afraid she might vomit. She let unconsciousness take her again.

When Jillian woke next, her mouth was no longer gagged, and her hands and feet were free, but she was lying awkwardly across the back seat of a vehicle, halfway on the floor, her face down and her body pressed by gravity against the back side of the front seat. When she tried to move, her head ached, but she tried to push herself up into a semi-sitting position anyway so she could figure out where she was.

Having become a morning person by habit after many months of working at the bakery, she knew that sunrise was shortly after seven at this time of the year. The sideways light of the rising sun shone through the windows, and it made her squint. She was thankful it wasn't full sunlight, which would've been much more painful. She groaned as she moved slowly. Even though it was her head that really hurt, every joint and muscle in her body seemed to object to any activity. How long she had lain there, she could only guess. It was probably only three hours since she had called Hunter. She hoped she hadn't lost an entire day or more, and she had no idea how far she was from Belle Haven.

She turned over so she could see through the back window. She could only see the sky and a few treetops. After she pushed herself up more so she could look through a side window, she realized that the vehicle was at the bottom of a steep ravine. Had she been in a car crash? She had no memory of it. She pulled herself up more to look over the back of the front seat. The driver wasn't moving and appeared to be unconscious, her forehead resting on the steering wheel. The airbag that had deployed was deflated beneath her. It was Avery.

Jillian reached over the seat to touch the side of her neck to see if there was a heartbeat. Her skin was cold, but there was a faint pulse. Jillian struggled out of her sweater and laid it across Avery's back, covering her as much as she could. It was the only thing she knew to do. She was afraid to try to move the other woman, not knowing what injuries she might have.

While she had no idea where they were or how they got there, she knew she had to get out and try to climb up to the road above if there was to be any hope for either of them. She tried to open one door and then the other, but both appeared to be locked and she couldn't get them to budge. She'd have to climb over the seat to the front and go out the passenger side. She moved slowly and carefully, not wanting to bump Avery and still very mindful of the pain in her head, until she was finally in the front seat and able to open the door.

The door swung open to its maximum width as the SUV was in an almost vertical position. She slid out feet first onto a rocky hillside. It was only then that she noticed that her clothing looked dusty and torn as if she'd been dragged through rough terrain, not unlike the hillside. Her forearms were covered with red scratches where they'd been exposed, and she only had one shoe on.

Using the length of the vehicle as a guide, she estimated that she would have to climb thirty or forty feet to get up to the level of the road. After climbing a few feet, it was evident her remaining soft-soled shoe provided little traction and almost no protection from the jagged edges of the rocks. But looking at her hands, which were scratched and dusty, she knew she was better off keeping the one shoe on. Even so, she lost it halfway up and watched it tumble back down to the bottom of the ravine, out of reach. She pressed on.

She didn't know how long it took, but she finally reached the level of the road. It appeared to be a little-used one, unpaved, with no guardrail along the steep side. The opposite side of the road was wooded. She couldn't see any buildings, and when she listened, she could only hear the sounds of birds and the rustle of the trees. She sat a few minutes, catching her breath, and then got up and started to walk in the direction that seemed to go downhill, though that was no guarantee it was the right direction toward civilization.

She realized she was thirsty and wished she'd checked the SUV for bottled water, but it was too late now. She wasn't about to climb back down, even for water. She felt somewhat faint, but she doggedly kept putting one foot in front of the other, knowing that if she stopped there was no guarantee that she would continue.

She finally reached a paved road, but still wasn't sure where she was. When she was a teenager, she'd known all the roads in Nathan County. She, Savannah, and James had taken turns driving down all the various roads just for fun after they'd gotten their licenses, but that had been years ago.

Fortunately, it wasn't long before a young man in a pickup truck came by. He used his cell phone to call 911 and stayed with Jillian until help arrived.

Sheriff Henderson was the first to arrive, followed closely by Laura Lee in a separate patrol car. An ambulance came about five minutes after that. Jillian was half expecting to have to answer questions, but after she told the sheriff the location of Avery's SUV, she was bundled straight into the ambulance and taken to the hospital.

After an examination and a CT scan, she was settled into a hospital bed, propped up with pillows. It wasn't long before Bertie arrived. She took one look at Jillian and tears welled up in her eyes, but she blinked them away. She carried a small overnight bag and her purse, both of which she placed in a chair before walking to Jillian and taking her hand. She laid a soft kiss on Jillian's left temple. When she spoke, Jillian could tell she was trying very hard to maintain her normal no-nonsense way of speaking, but emotion still filled her voice.

"The scrapes you get into, child. Now, before you ask, Cornelia's at home with Bonnie. They both wanted to come, but we decided it would be better for Bonnie not to come to the hospital. We didn't want her to see you like this, and I can see that was a good decision."

Jillian had yet to look in a mirror, so she wasn't aware of how she looked.

Bertie continued. "Hunter insisted on driving me over. He's waiting out in the hallway. He's been worried sick since he called Gooder about five this morning and found out you hadn't talked to him. That's when we discovered you were missing. He was over to Belle Haven like a shot."

Jillian touched her hair, wondering what it must look like. One of the nurses had cleaned her face, and it had stung.

"Is that bag for me? I don't suppose you brought a mirror and a hairbrush?"

Bertie got up to retrieve the bag. "I just stuck a few things in here. I wasn't sure how long you'd have to stay." She brought it to Jillian. "The doctor told us he wants you to stay a few hours for observation, and then you can come home."

Jillian looked inside the bag, found a brush and a handheld mirror, and gave the bag back to Bertie. She laid the brush down and was silent several moments while she looked in the mirror at the bruise on her forehead and the directional scratches on the right side of her face that went across her nose, forehead, and cheek. They seemed superficial, but she couldn't help wondering if there would be scars. Try as she might, she couldn't remember how she'd gotten them. "Have you heard anything about Avery's condition?"

Bertie took the brush and began gently brushing the ends of Jillian's long red hair. "No. They won't tell us anything, except that she's alive. A special team had to be called out to extract her from the SUV. Her husband's been called. That's all I know. When you feel up to it, I'm sure Coy will come to talk to you." Bertie had known the sheriff since he was a boy, and she rarely referred to him by his official title.

"It didn't seem like it took that long for help to come after that young man called 911—I didn't even get his name—or for the ambulance to get to the hospital from there."

"Well, the police went searching for you as soon as we realized you were missing, so I know Laura Lee and Gooder were already out patrolling. Coy assigned that young feller, you know—tall, skinny, his dad has a pecan farm over near Painter's Ridge—Shaw, that's it, Tom Shaw. He's been assigned to stay at Belle Haven to keep an eye on things. They—the police—combed Belle Haven from top to bottom. Found your phone on the front porch. Anyway, so they were out looking for you all the time."

"So where exactly were we?"

"Coy called Hunter when he got to your location. He said it was about eight miles from Belle Haven, just off of Route 18."

"Only eight miles?"

"Yes. Does that not seem right?"

"Honestly, Bertie, I can't remember much. I was knocked out. I woke up once and it was dark, and I was tied up. When I woke the second time, everything was different. It was light outside, and I was in Avery's SUV. But I don't think that's where I was the first time. Or maybe I only imagined being tied up. I just don't know." Her head started to ache, and she closed her eyes and reached up to rub her forehead, forgetting about the bruise and the scratches. She winced.

Bertie laid down the brush on the side table. "Don't you worry about any of that right now. You just need to rest. Let your memories come back on their own."

"But the sheriff will want to know. He'll need to know so that he can figure this out. I'm so confused, I—"

"You stop it right now." Bertie took the mirror off Jillian's lap and laid it next to the brush. "You close your eyes and rest. I asked the doctor if I needed to keep you awake, and he said no, they don't recommend that anymore for concussions, except to check every couple of hours. So you just clear your mind and try to sleep. I forbid you to even think of anything remotely stressful until you feel better."

Jillian knew that tone. There was only one reply Bertie would accept. "Yes, ma'am."

"Before you drift off, though, I think Hunter wants to see you. I'll allow that." Bertie went out the door and Jillian heard her call his name.

Hunter was at Jillian's bedside in less than a minute. Bertie had remained in the hallway. He was visibly shocked when he first saw her, but recovered quickly. He reached out to hold her hand, but seemed at a loss for words. Finally he asked, "Can I get you anything?"

"No. I'm okay. The doctor told Bertie I can go home in a few hours."

He shook his head. "I'm sorry this happened to you. I should have come over when you called. If only I'd—"

Jillian interrupted. "Hunter, don't. I doubt it would have made any difference. I never even made it inside the house after I finished talking to you."

"Even so. I'll never let this happen again. I promise."

"It's not your fault, Hunter. Please don't blame yourself."

He was about to respond when a nurse entered the room to check on Jillian. "She needs to rest."

Hunter let go of Jillian's hand reluctantly. "I'll be in the waiting room just down the hall if you need anything." He leaned over and gave her a gentle kiss on the cheek before leaving the room.

After Hunter's departure, Bertie returned and made herself comfortable in the chair, retrieving her reading glasses, an ink pen, and a folded newspaper from her purse. Jillian watched as she started to write in what she knew was the daily crossword puzzle, since Bertie worked that every day except Sunday. She closed her eyes and didn't know anything else until a nurse came in to take her vitals, just before noon.

After eating a small bowl of green gelatin and some cottage cheese, Jillian was allowed to get dressed in order to head on home to Belle Haven. Bertie assured her that she was going to eat more than that when she got home, sounding like that would be the case whether Jillian wanted to or not. The image of Bertie rustling up lunch in the kitchen made her remember that Bertie was not at the bakery.

"Oh no. What about the bakery? Is it closed again today?" She was thinking about the loss of income.

"It's covered. Abram and Henry headed home yesterday so that Abram could get back to work and Henry to school. Dorie's going to stay a couple more days to help Lenora at the bakery. I arranged it with them yesterday after Patricia asked me to judge."

"Why didn't you tell me that?"

"Oh I don't know. There didn't seem to be time, and you were so distracted yesterday, I just didn't."

"Did it ever occur to you that I might be distracted about who was going to work the bakery while you were playing judge and I was looking after Bonnie?"

"No it didn't. Was that what you were distracted about?"

"Well, no. It didn't even cross my mind, to tell the truth. It was those darned books."

"Then why raise a ruckus? And what 'darned' books are you referring to?"

"The children's books I found in the attic. They were missing, and then I found them, and now someone's swiped them again."

Bertie narrowed her eyes. She seemed to be about to ask a question and thought the better of it. "Well, whatever. I'm sure they'll turn up."

Jillian decided to just drop the subject. Her head was starting to ache again. "Does Dorie know what to do at the bakery?"

"Of course she does. She's been baking with her mother since she was a little thing. Lenora will tell her whatever else she needs to know. They'll have a nice time working together."

Jillian could only think, *At least one thing has worked out for the best.*

A short time after that, Hunter drove Bertie and Jillian home. He was silent, and his expression was grim. Jillian feared that he was still blaming himself for what had happened to her. She didn't know what else she could say to reassure him, so she was quiet too. At Belle Haven, he parked in the porte cochere and saw them to the back door. He took his leave, promising to look in on her soon.

Jillian and Bertie headed straight to Bertie's main-floor bedroom where she insisted Jillian would stay for the next several days. The doctor had warned Jillian that she should avoid hitting her head again at all costs, and Bertie had already forbidden her to use the stairs until she began to feel a whole lot better.

It was a good arrangement since the last thing Jillian wanted was to see a bunch of people, or to be seen by them. Before she saw Aunt Cornelia and Bonnie, she wanted to have a chance to get herself together—a shower, a change of clothes, maybe even some makeup. Just something to make her feel normal again.

Bertie's bedroom had once been the servants' quarters, situated as it was near the kitchen. Remodeled since then to be a master suite, it included a private bathroom and a sitting area with a small fireplace, now with a gas insert. The sitting area was furnished with two comfortable wingback chairs, each with a matching ottoman, and a small table and floor lamp between the chairs. One chair had been her grandfather's. Now his ottoman served as a holding place for a stack of magazines and books, and the seat of his chair held a folded soft woven throw with fringed edges and a couple of extra pillows.

Bertie's bed was covered with a wedding-ring quilt that had been a twenty-fifth wedding anniversary present given to them by Genevieve. It had spent years tucked away in a trunk, put there after the death of her husband when Jillian was still a teenager, until one day last year, Bertie had decided it should once again be used so she could enjoy the beauty of it and the memories it held.

While Bertie went upstairs to get some clothing and other necessities for her, Jillian took a leisurely shower. Afterward, she gently dried her hair with a towel before combing it and then fluffing it out with her fingers to let it fall into its naturally curly state rather than trying to tame it as she normally did. When she came out of the bathroom, some of her clothes plus a square basket full of her toiletries and her makeup bag had been placed on the bed. A few articles of her clothing were hanging on the wire rack on the back of the bedroom door. She considered and then bypassed the nightgown Bertie had brought down and instead selected a loose, short-sleeved beige dress with large front pockets that fell just below the knee.

She grabbed the tube of prescription-strength antibiotic ointment a nurse had given for her scratches from the overnight bag plus the makeup bag from the basket, and then sat down on the narrow bench at Bertie's vanity table, an antique with a large attached round mirror. The scratches were still quite red on her face, but the nurse had told her if she kept them clean and used the ointment regularly, they would soon heal and fade as they were not deep. She considered trying to conceal them with some makeup, but decided that probably didn't count as keeping them clean. She'd just have to live with it. She dabbed the ointment on her face and forearms, and then put on some eye shadow and liner and a light coating of lipstick. It made her feel marginally better.

There was a light knock on the door.

Jillian looked once more at her image. She'd done what she could. She turned away from the mirror and sat facing the door. "Come in."

Cornelia came in, ushering Bonnie in front of her. Jillian could tell by Bonnie's expression that Bertie had tried to prepare her for how Jillian looked. The first thing Bonnie did was to come over and give her a warm hug, placing her head on Jillian's chest. Jillian hugged her back and traded a meaningful look with Cornelia over the little girl's head.

Bonnie stepped back to look at Jillian's face. "Does it hurt?"

"Only a little. I'll be better soon."

"Mama's coming to get me tomorrow, but I'll ask her if I can stay if you need me."

Jillian had forgotten that this would be Bonnie's last night at Belle Haven for the foreseeable future. A small lump formed in her throat. "That is sweet of you to offer, Bonnie, but you should go with your mother. I'm sure she and your daddy miss you very much. Miss Bertie and Miss Cornelia will take good care of me."

Bonnie looked around the room. "Are we sleeping in here tonight?"

Cornelia spoke up. "Maybe you should sleep with Miss Bertie in Miss Jillian's bedroom tonight, where you're used to being."

Bonnie looked at Jillian, waiting to see what she would say.

"I think Bonnie and I will be fine together down here," said Jillian. "I wouldn't want to miss our last night together, and we have the last two chapters of *A Little Princess* to read. Do you remember where we were?"

"The man who had been looking for Sara for two years finally found her, and she was just on the other side of the wall all that time!"

Jillian smiled. "You have been listening."

There was another knock on the door. The door opened before Jillian could answer, and Bertie peeked in. "Jillian, Coy is here, and he wants to know if he can talk to you. Do you feel up to it? If you don't, I'll tell him to wait until tomorrow."

"No, it's okay. I want to help all I can. Should I come out there?" She stood up.

"It'll be more private in here." Bertie walked over to the chairs by the fireplace, picked up the magazines and books, and put them on the dresser. Then she moved the throw and pillows to the end of the bed. "He can sit in Jack's chair."

Cornelia walked over to give Jillian a kiss on her unscratched cheek. "It's good to have you home, Jillian. Let me know if you need anything."

"I will, Aunt Cornelia. Thanks."

Sheriff Henderson must have been right outside the door, because as soon as Bertie, Cornelia, and Bonnie had vacated the room, he entered, carrying his hat in one hand and a notebook in the other. Jillian indicated he should sit in her grandfather's chair, and she took Bertie's. After he laid his hat on the ottoman, he took out a pencil and poised it above the notebook that rested on his right leg. He was an old-school law officer. No recorders or computer tablets for him.

"Take your time and just try to tell me everything that happened from the time you discovered Mrs. Hadley was gone from Belle Haven until the time you flagged down that pickup truck driver."

She told him everything she could remember, even the things that she wasn't sure were real after she was hit on the head. After she had reached the last detail, and he had put away his pencil, she asked about Avery.

"She's still unconscious. We do know that she was drugged."

"Drugged? Does that mean she didn't leave here on her own accord?"

"It doesn't look like it. The forensics people haven't finished going over Mrs. Hadley's SUV. It took a while to get it out of that ravine after she was extracted from it. I don't hold out much hope for finding any evidence in the vehicle, but, you never know, we may get lucky and find something that will help us. Whoever is behind this is cagey—and careful. The only fingerprints we found on the poisoned bottle of sherry were Mrs. Hadley's, so it's likely the suspect wiped it clean after adding the rat poison."

"Rat poison? I thought it was cyanide."

"The lab tests showed that it was cyanide in an old rat poison formulation. They don't make it like that anymore. We found several packets in a box in the garden shed that probably should have been disposed of decades ago. Cornelia said the box had been in the barn, and that she moved it to the shed when renovations were begun. We cleared it all out to check it for fingerprints, but whoever did this was careful, like I said—and an opportunist."

"What do you mean?"

"None of it seems to be premeditated. Mrs. Woods told us her spice labels had been switched, but no one else said that anything had happened to them. I suspect the person who did that was the same one who poisoned the sherry. She, or he, found Mrs. Wood's bedroom door open or unlocked, and saw the jars and switched the labels on the spur of the moment. The rat poison was on the property, not something brought in by the perpetrator. Mrs. Hadley was drugged with over-the-counter medication. We searched your guests' luggage again this morning and found nothing of that sort, but I asked Bertie to check her stores, and she found that there were a couple of things missing from the upstairs medicine cabinet."

"So you don't think Avery had anything to do with the poisoning?"

"I've thought from the beginning that she was the likely target, and now, with what happened last night and this morning . . ." He didn't confirm his conclusions on the matter. "Thing is, poisons and overdoses are normally the modus operandi of women, but moving you from the front porch took some strength. That points to a man."

"Or to two people."

"Yes, that's also a possibility."

Jillian's next question sprang from a logical progression. "What about the Oglethorpes—Florence and Charles? Are they still in town?"

"I was going to give them the okay to head back to Atlanta today if they wanted to. After Jones reported that you and Mrs. Hadley were missing this morning, I sent Deputy Zane to the Southern Peach Inn where they're staying. She said it looked like they were ready to check out—bags packed and all that. She put a stop to it." He shook his head, looking exhausted. "I'd arrest and throw every last one of them in jail if I could. It would help if I had a decent motive."

"The only motive I can think of," said Jillian, "is to ruin the production of this TV show, but I don't see how it could possibly benefit anyone. Houston, Victor, and Patricia are the only ones who really knew each other before, and they all have a vested interest in having it succeed. The others were complete strangers as far as I can tell. And Florence obviously hoped it would lead to bigger and better things. And why the focus on Avery? Because she was the best baker? It doesn't add up, Sheriff Henderson. I suppose there could be a revenge angle, but . . ." Jillian started to shake her head, but stopped immediately when it throbbed unpleasantly.

"I think that's enough for now," Henderson said, seeing her discomfort. He stood and thanked Jillian for her help, and was about to leave. "There's one more thing. I've already talked about this with Bertie. I had intended to meet with this group this morning, but with everything that's happened, I put it off. So instead, I'll be talking to them this afternoon at three here at Belle Haven. I'd like you to be available, if you feel up to it."

Jillian started to say she'd rather not, but he continued.

"You don't have to say anything. I mainly want you to listen and see if everything you hear rings true. I know they've only been here a few days, but I imagine you've gotten to know them as well as anyone could in that period of time. Cornelia and Bertie are sitting in too, so please consider it. It could help."

With that he took his leave. Jillian sank back into the soft chair and put her feet up. In a few seconds she was asleep.

When Jillian woke, she found that someone, Bertie or Cornelia, had covered her with the soft throw and slid a pillow between her head and the wing of the chair. On her grandfather's ottoman there was a tray that held a plate with a sandwich and a dill-pickle spear, a small bowl of mixed berries with cream, and a large glass of iced sweet tea. The ice was still intact, so it had not been there long.

Grateful to be in a place where there was someone to look to her well-being, Jillian said a quick prayer before digging into the meal, finding that she was famished. When she was finished, she got up and carried the tray into the kitchen. Cornelia was there.

"Thanks for lunch. It really hit the spot."

"Sleep and good food are the best medicine. We'll have you back to one hundred percent before you know it."

"Where are Bertie and Bonnie?"

"Bertie went upstairs to take a nap. Savannah came by to see you, but since you were asleep, she offered to take Bonnie out for ice cream. She said they wouldn't be gone too long."

Jillian sat down on a stool at the island counter and listened for a moment. The house seemed fairly quiet. "Where is everyone else?"

"I'm not sure, but last I looked, Chester was reading in the library, and Dorothea and Kaylee were in the living room. I haven't seen Waldon since lunchtime, so he could be upstairs in his room. Patricia, Houston, and Victor went out to the barn a little while ago. Patricia said she's going to have the crew pack up and move on to the next venue. I think it's more of a hopeful gesture than anything else. I don't see how they can continue the series until whoever is behind this is exposed."

"Well, there goes Bertie's moment in the sun. I guess she won't get to be on TV after all."

The front doorbell rang. Jillian automatically started to rise. Cornelia put her hand out to stop her. "You stay put. I'll get it."

Half a minute after Cornelia left the kitchen, Savannah and Bonnie came in through the back door. Savannah gave Jillian a gentle hug, and then stepped back to look her over.

"Well, I've seen you look better—and worse."

"Such as?"

"That time you wanted to dye your hair auburn, and it turned out green instead. As I recall, your mom made you soak your hair in tomato juice for hours. Messy, but it did help a little. She called you 'Anne Girl' for a month after that."

"Why did she call her that?" asked Bonnie.

"Because the same thing happened to Anne Shirley in *Anne of Green Gables*. She was a redhead too."

Bonnie giggled. "Was it really green?"

Jillian rolled her eyes. "I'm afraid so. Thank you, friend, for reminding me of that."

Savannah grinned. "That's what old friends are for."

"What other embarrassing stories have you been telling Bonnie about me?"

"Oh, we talked about all kinds of things. You weren't always the topic of conversation."

Bonnie climbed up on the stool next to Jillian with her legs folded beneath her and put her elbows on the counter with her hands clasped together. She leaned toward Jillian and in a stage whisper said, "I'll tell you later."

Cornelia walked back into the kitchen carrying a footed glass vase filled with an arrangement of peach-colored roses. "A delivery for you, Jillian, from the flower shop." She set the vase on the counter in front of Jillian.

Bonnie stretched over to touch one of the rose petals with the tip of her finger. "These flowers are beautiful, Miss Jillian. They're just like you."

Jillian just smiled at her remark. The little girl was so good for her morale. She asked Cornelia, "Who are they from?"

"I didn't look at the card. I wanted to, but I refrained. Still, I have my suspicions."

Jillian reached up and grabbed the little envelope that was stuck in the top of the arrangement. She opened it and read the card.

"Well?" asked Savannah. "Is it from whom I think it is?"

Jillian nodded and simply said, "It's from Hunter." She put the card back in the envelope and tucked it in her pocket.

At three o'clock, everyone associated with the TV show, except Avery, had gathered in the living room of Belle Haven: Patricia, Victor, Houston, Chester, Waldon, Dorothea, and Kaylee, plus Florence and her husband, Charles. Bertie, Cornelia, and Jillian sat at the periphery of the group. Jillian began to feel like she had stumbled into that overused film scene where the detective says, "I suppose you're all wondering why I called you here this evening." Then he'd give a long speech to build suspense and finally announce the culprit. The problem was, Jillian was pretty sure that Sheriff Henderson didn't know who the guilty party was. She certainly didn't.

Savannah had offered to look after Bonnie during the meeting, so they went outside for a walk in the garden. That left Jillian free to concentrate on what she was about to hear. She'd brought a small notebook and pencil with her so she could make notes about what was said as well as what was left unsaid.

Sheriff Henderson, who was a man of imposing stature, stood in front of the fireplace where he could see the faces of everyone in the room. Deputy Shaw was there as well, across the room from Henderson, standing in the middle of the doorway with his arms crossed. Jillian had to admit the effect of two officers standing in full uniform, guns at their sides, was intimidating, and she wasn't even guilty of anything. But she supposed that was the point—an attempt to intimidate the culprit into making a mistake.

Sheriff Henderson began. "I've interviewed each of you individually, but now, we're going to do this as a group. I may be asking many of the same questions that you've already answered, but even so, I want you to answer again, not leaving out any details. I'll know if you do."

He began with general questions about their arrivals in Moss Hollow, how they were selected to be on the show, and if they had known each other previously. A lot of the information was new to Jillian, but she could see why Henderson wanted her there. Dorothea's nervousness could be mistaken for guilt, but Jillian knew from experience that it was her typical reaction to stress. Patricia could seem cold and calculating, but Jillian was certain it was a façade she'd learned to get by in the business world. She'd seen Patricia's softer side, so she knew it was there.

She went on listening to the answers and comments, seeing each person through the lenses of the personalities she'd come to know. She made a few notes. The meeting had gone on for about an hour when Jillian could see that Florence was starting to get steamed up. It would be just a matter of time before she blew.

She proved Jillian right minutes later. "I don't know why Charles and I have to be here and answer all these ridiculous questions," Florence said in a louder voice than was necessary.

Jillian began to wonder if she might be slightly deaf, but then, she'd never noticed that Florence had trouble hearing other people, even Waldon, who had the quietest voice among the guests. *No, she just wants to make sure she's noticed, no matter what the situation.*

"I've already told you who's behind all this," Florence continued. She pointed at Patricia. "That woman is a fraud and vindictive to boot. She tried to get rid of me because I know the truth about her, and I can prove it."

Henderson was cool as a cucumber. "You've said as much, but I've yet to see any proof."

"That's because that woman," she turned and pointed at Jillian, "searched my property without my consent. She should be arrested."

Jillian and Bertie glanced at each other, but neither spoke. When Jillian looked back at Henderson, she could tell he'd noticed the look they'd exchanged. He took a deep breath and seemed to be considering his next move. He looked at Florence.

"Are you accusing Miss Green of stealing something that belonged to you?"

Florence fidgeted a moment. "Not exactly." She turned a look on her husband that seemed to say, *This is all your fault.* Jillian figured he'd probably been raked over the coals for not collecting the luggage from Florence's room himself. "But I know she was in my luggage."

"Miss Green, did you remove something from Mrs. Oglethorpe's luggage?"

"I did remove something, but it was my property, not hers. Her husband called and requested that I collect her things and have them ready for him to pick up at the front door. Her suitcase was not zipped. I only opened it to place a piece of her clothing inside. That's when I saw the yellow booklet that belongs to me, or at least to Belle Haven, and I removed it."

Florence jumped up from her chair and pointed at Jillian again. "You see! She admits that she removed evidence! Arrest her!"

Sheriff Henderson gave Florence a hard stare. "Mrs. Oglethorpe, take your seat. If you don't settle down, I'll have no choice but to have Deputy Shaw take you down to the station and put you in jail. Do you understand me?"

Jillian wasn't sure if that was an empty threat or not. She tended to think not. Sheriff Henderson wasn't the empty-threat type.

Charles put his hand on Florence's arm. She gave Jillian a hateful look and sat down. "I understand."

"Miss Green. Do you have this booklet in your possession?"

"Yes, sheriff."

"Would you please bring it to me?"

"Of course."

In just a couple of minutes, Jillian had retrieved the yellow booklet from her desk and returned to the living room. As she crossed the room toward Sheriff Henderson, Florence leaped out of her chair and made a beeline toward Jillian, almost knocking her over in her attempt to grab the booklet. She would've succeeded, both in knocking Jillian over and getting the book, but, fortunately, Henderson was quick on his feet and moved to steady Jillian, at the same time placing himself between the two women.

"That does it!" he roared. "Shaw! Take this woman and her husband down to the station. Book her for assault and attempted extortion and anything else you can think of."

"You can't do that to me!" Florence shouted. "I'm the victim here." Jabbing a finger at Patricia, she screamed, "She tried to kill me!" Then she turned her vehemence on Jillian, who was trembling from another near fall. "And she tried to keep me from getting what I deserve."

"Believe me, Mrs. Oglethorpe, you will be getting what you deserve. Take her, Shaw."

Charles got up quickly and put a hand on Florence's arm, as she started to say something else that would no doubt hurt her situation even more. "It'll be all right, Florence. I'll call our lawyer. Please, let's just go."

Jillian could tell Florence was ready to argue with him, but was rendered speechless when Deputy Shaw approached her with handcuffs.

"Surely there's no need for those," said Charles.

"That's up to her, sir," replied Shaw.

Florence looked furious and didn't answer immediately, but finally said, "I'll go. And without the handcuffs."

Shaw looked at Henderson, and he gave a nod to indicate they could do without the handcuffs.

When they finally left the room, Henderson helped Jillian to her chair. "You okay?" There was deep concern in his voice.

Jillian was still shaking, but she said, "Yes."

Henderson accepted the yellow booklet from her. He walked back over to the fireplace and flipped through the booklet quickly before placing it on the mantel behind him.

"Now, where were we before that outburst?" he asked.

"Why do we have to go on?" asked Chester. "It seems pretty obvious that Florence and her husband were behind everything."

"Because I don't believe for a second that Mrs. Oglethorpe poisoned herself. She had no reason to, and she could have died. Also, she had other plans that would not coincide with stopping the production of the TV show." He exchanged a look with Patricia.

"What about that booklet?" asked Kaylee. "What's up with that?"

"That's another matter that we will be looking into," said Henderson. "But the subject at hand is more serious. Besides the poisoning, there are the attacks on Mrs. Hadley and Miss Green. Mrs. Hadley is still unconscious. Before it's all said and done, this could still turn out to be a murder investigation." Sheriff Henderson turned toward Jillian. "Is there anything you can think of that we haven't covered here? It could be the smallest thing."

Jillian thought back over the past week and tried to remember what had happened each day. It was a lot to go through. Suddenly it dawned on her. "Oh, the books. The missing children's books."

"What children's books?"

"Savannah and I found some old children's books in the attic a few days before Bonnie came to stay. Then last, um . . ." Jillian paused, trying to remember the day. "It was last Saturday night, I think. That's when I noticed they were missing the first time. Then I forgot about them until I found them in the armoire in the attic. After that, I hid them in a trunk in my bedroom, but someone found them and took them again."

"So at present, you don't know where they are?"

"No."

"Were they valuable?"

Jillian shrugged her shoulders. "I don't really know. I wouldn't think so. They just have sentimental value."

There was an uncomfortable silence and the sheriff looked at the faces around the room. "Do any of you know anything about these books? Mr. Dale, you run a bookstore in Key West, don't you?"

Chester looked like a deer caught in headlights. "I do, but I don't carry any children's books in my store. I have a pretty, um, selective clientele. I carry a lot of modern fiction, Hemmingway, Steinbeck, Bellow, and postmoderns like Rushdie and Pynchon—that sort of thing. And I have nonfiction—travel, politics, history. But it's all aimed at adults, not kids."

"Okay. Who else?" Henderson looked around the room. When no one spoke, he looked at his notes. "Mr. Radcliffe, you've said you're an antiquarian. What exactly is it that you do? Do you deal in books?"

Waldon nodded. "I have dealt in old books and manuscripts, but those of a very old nature—late Middle Ages mostly, some early American. But I'm really drawn more to antiques from the Victorian era—furniture, art, and things that were in common use such as writing and vanity sets, watches." He reached in his pocket, pulled out a business card, and handed it to the sheriff. "My specialties are listed on my card."

Sheriff Henderson glanced at the front and back of the card before putting it in his shirt pocket. He looked at his notes again. "Ms. Sinclair, you're a veterinary nurse. Do you know anything about these missing books?"

"No, sir," said Kaylee. "I mean, I saw them like everybody else the first day we got here, but I have no real interest in them. And I never saw anyone take them."

Sheriff Henderson sighed audibly. "Mrs. Woods, you're a kindergarten teacher. You must have an interest in children's books."

Jillian couldn't help feeling sorry for Dorothea. The woman was easily unnerved, and her voice waivered as she spoke. "Of course I have an interest in children's books. I recognized all the titles of the books except for one. I don't know what their value is beyond being excellent books to read. I'm an honest person, and I would never, ever steal anything. My parents taught me better than that. I'm using my sick days to stay here, you know, and it's not easy for my family nor for my students. Believe me, if I knew anything about what's happened, I would tell you. I just want to go home. This is the worst experience of my life." She was near to tears when she finished.

Jillian looked across at Patricia, who put her head down, looking distraught.

"All right. I understand," said Sheriff Henderson. "And believe me, I will release you to go home as soon as possible. Does anyone else have anything to add?"

He hadn't asked Patricia, Houston, or Victor about the books. Jillian supposed that meant he had reduced his list of suspects to the four contestants and wondered if he was making a mistake ruling out anyone—even Florence. What better way to deflect suspicion than to put yourself in the position of a victim? Maybe she knew there was just enough in the swig of sherry to make her sick but not kill her, and maybe that was why she had asked for it. It would make sense if she'd known how concentrated the poison was, and it was a smart way to control how much she got. With a shudder, Jillian felt somewhat better knowing that at least Florence and Charles were no longer free to make mischief.

But that didn't mean that there wasn't still someone under her roof who was, as Sheriff Henderson had said, an "opportunist," just looking for a chance to cause trouble.

Bertie and Cornelia refused to allow Jillian to have anything to do with fixing supper that evening, so she lay down to take another nap after Sheriff Henderson left. Bertie had packed up all of Bonnie's clothes in her suitcase and brought it and Mr. Benjamin downstairs since they had traded bedrooms. Seeing the suitcase lying on the vanity's bench and Mr. Benjamin propped up in the corner of Bertie's chair made Jillian feel broody as she lay on the bed curled up with a pillow. She thought of how quickly she had adjusted to having the little girl be a part of her life, and how much she would miss her when she left.

Lilith had called earlier to confirm that she would be arriving late the following morning to pick up Bonnie. She also told them that she was bringing her mother, Margaret, and grandmother, Genevieve, for a visit, and Bertie immediately asked them to stay for lunch at Belle Haven. After the call, Bertie had told their other guests that they would be on their own for that meal.

Later on, when Jillian got up and stepped out of the bedroom, she could hear activity and voices from the kitchen, including Bonnie's, so she headed to her office to check her e-mail. The young police officer, who had previously introduced himself as Deputy Tom Shaw, was on duty in the foyer. He nodded at her as she walked by, but said nothing.

Patricia's crew had been working all afternoon to pack up their equipment from the hall, so, for the first time in days, there was no need for a night watchman there, but she was glad for the presence of the police in Belle Haven tonight. *At least I don't have to pay this one*, she thought.

She didn't remain long in her office. Staring at the computer screen only served to bring on a slight headache. She put it in sleep mode before her headache got any worse and wandered into the kitchen. Bonnie was at the island counter, standing on a footstool and brushing melted butter over unbaked biscuits, wearing a bib apron that fit her perfectly. It had been made with a vintage fabric that had a deep-yellow background covered with tiny blue and red flowers, and the apron had red trim and red ties at the neck and waist. It looked vaguely familiar.

"Where did you get the apron?" she asked Bertie.

"Don't you remember? I made it for you when you were little. I dug it out from the bottom drawer of the china cabinet day before yesterday and washed and pressed it. I thought Bonnie might like to take it with her when she goes if that's all right with you. She's grown quite attached to it."

Jillian smiled. "Of course. I think that would be very nice."

"Did you really used to wear this, Miss Jillian?" Bonnie asked.

"I did, and now it will be yours to wear when you help your mother and father around the house."

Bonnie dipped the brush in the container of melted butter and dribbled butter across the counter before painting what remained across the top of a biscuit. "Mama never makes biscuits like this at home. Miss Bertie said she would teach me how the next time I come to visit, and then I can teach Mama. She said she would practice on me so that when she had her own great-grandchildren, she could teach them too."

Cornelia chuckled. Jillian looked at Bertie, who tried to look perfectly innocent, as if she hadn't encouraged Bonnie to bring up that particular topic. She didn't succeed.

After dinner that evening, Jillian was shooed away again, forbidden to help with cleanup. She wandered around downstairs for a bit, but felt awkward in the company of her guests now, and the feeling seemed to be mutual. She went back to Bertie's bedroom and tried to read a book for a while, but she couldn't concentrate. She tried looking at a magazine, but she found nothing that captured her attention. She finally gave up and made her way to the kitchen.

The kitchen was clean, and the dishwasher whirred. She found Bertie sitting at the table in the breakfast nook with Bonnie in the chair next to her, kneeling so she could see what Bertie held. In the middle of the table were two large shoe boxes, one with the lid removed, revealing that it was full of photographs. In front of Bertie were a couple of stacks of old black-and-white pictures.

"Are you looking for something special or just perusing?" asked Jillian.

"I decided to go through these this evening to see if I could find some old pictures of Genevieve when she came to visit Belle Haven as a little girl and also as a young woman," answered Bertie. "I thought Bonnie might like to see them, and Lilith and Margaret might like to have some of the pictures or make copies if they don't already have them. Particularly Lilith, since they're going to be so far away. It's important to remember where you came from."

"Where's Aunt Cornelia?"

Bertie suddenly wore half a grin, but continued to sort through the photos without looking up. "She's gone out to the movies. There's a special showing of *Casablanca* down at the Cinema Four." She glanced at the wall clock. "She ought to be back soon.

They went to the early showing right after supper. Some of our guests helped with the cleanup, so it wasn't a problem."

"Did you say 'they'?" Jillian raised her eyebrows, forgetting that it was slightly painful to do so, and quickly returned them to their normal position.

"Yes I did. Burton asked her to go with him. Of course she had to drive her car and pick him up since he doesn't drive after dark anymore, but she didn't seem to mind." She glanced up at Jillian, the grin now full-size.

The subject was dropped when Bonnie asked, "Who is that?" and pointed at the picture Bertie held.

"That's your grandmamma Genevieve and her older brother, Lonnie. He was your great-great uncle. This picture was taken in front of the double doors that lead to the library. See?"

Jillian walked around the table to look at the photo over Bertie's shoulder. She recognized Belle Haven's library doors. Then she concentrated on the two children, who were holding hands and appeared to be not much older than Bonnie was now. They had such similar features, it was clear they were brother and sister. Their clothing was perfectly pressed, not a wrinkle to be seen. The girl had ribbons tied in her hair and wore a short dress with two wide ruffles around the hem. The boy wore a bow tie at the collar of his white shirt and a pair of check-patterned shorts. The girl looked like she was on the verge of a smile, and the boy looked like he just wanted it to be over with.

"Lonnie was killed in the war—World War II. He was a pilot." Bertie's expression showed she was sorting through old memories along with the old photos. "Cornelia and I weren't much older than Bonnie when he died, but I remember him. He was so handsome, and smart too. Such a wa—" She stopped herself abruptly.

"Such a what?" asked Jillian.

"I started to say, 'such a waste,' but none of those sacrifices were a waste. They were fighting against something that was evil, and sometimes that has to be done. How does that quote go? 'Evil succeeds when good men do nothing?' Lonnie was one of those young men who did something, even at the cost of his own life." She picked up another photo and handed it to Jillian. "Here he is in the cockpit of his plane in his flight suit. I remember Genevieve brought us this photo when she came to stay with us a few days during the war when Mama and Daddy were away."

Jillian looked at the young man in the photo. He was wearing a leather helmet with goggles, and the parachute on his back was visible. She thought he had the same impatient expression on his face as he had in the other picture: "Are we done yet?"

Jillian sat down in the chair on the other side of Bonnie. She reached for a stack of photos that Bertie had set aside. "Do you mind if I look too? It's been a while since I went through any of the old photos around here. I don't even recall seeing these before."

Bertie found more photos of Genevieve at different stages of her early life, including one of her as a young mother, sitting in the living room of Belle Haven on the old horsehair sofa that was now in Jillian's office. She held the baby Margaret in her arms.

It must have been hours later that Jillian looked up from the photos and noticed Bonnie yawning. She glanced at the wall clock and realized that it was way past Bonnie's usual bedtime. Jillian then remembered that she had intended to ask Bertie earlier to bring down *A Little Princess* so she could read the final chapters to Bonnie.

She put down the stack of photos she'd been looking at and stood up. "Bonnie, I think it's time we got ready for bed. I'm just going to go up and get *A Little Princess* from my nightstand."

"No you are not." Bertie started to stand up.

Bonnie put her little hand on Bertie's arm. "May I go up and get it? I know right where it is."

Bertie settled back down in her chair. "I think that's a fine idea."

Bonnie seemed to have regained some energy and hopped down from the chair. "I'll be right back."

Jillian sat back down at the table. "You know, I'll have to use the stairs eventually. I'm really feeling much better."

"You will wait a few days before you go up those stairs again," said Bertie. "The doctor said not to take any chances with a fall, and that's just what we're going to do. I was ready to flatten that Florence woman when she almost knocked you over. It was a good thing Coy stepped in, or I would have."

Jillian didn't doubt that for a moment, and she knew Florence had gotten off easy with the sheriff's interference instead of Bertie's. She opened her mouth to speak, but Bertie put up her hand.

"And there'll be no argument about those stairs."

Jillian picked up some photos again and started looking through them. She asked a few questions about who people were and was amazed sometimes to find that she knew them now, but hadn't recognized them as youngsters.

Cornelia entered through the back door. Jillian couldn't help but smile at the pains her aunt had taken with her appearance to go to the movies with Burton Puckett. She wore a chiffon dress with a flowery print that reminded Jillian of a painting by Monet. She had a long scarf in a complementary color draped around her neck and wore shoes that matched it. She was a picture of elegance. All she needed was a wide-brimmed hat and white gloves, and she would've been dressed perfectly for a tea party with the Queen of England.

Jillian couldn't resist asking. "Did you have a good time at the movie?"

Cornelia raised an eyebrow. "Of course. Humphrey Bogart, Ingrid Bergman, Paul Henreid—what's not to love? It's always been one of my favorite movies."

"That's not what I meant, and you know it."

"Burton was fine."

"Just fine?"

"Yes. Just fine. I have to say, he's improved since he was a teenager." She glanced over the photos now spread across the table and changed the subject. "I see you found the photograph boxes. Any luck finding pictures of Genevieve?"

Without a word, Bertie handed her the stack of the photos she had found.

As Cornelia started to look at the pictures, she asked, "Has Bonnie already gone to bed?"

Jillian glanced up at the clock, surprised to see that fifteen minutes had passed since Bonnie left the table to go upstairs. She stood up.

"She went to get *A Little Princess* from my bedside. She should have been back down here a while ago."

Cornelia read the look on Jillian's face and put down the photos on the table. "You stay put. I'll go see what she's gotten into."

After everything that had happened the last few days, Jillian's mind went into overdrive. Instead of staying put as ordered, she followed Cornelia to the bottom of the staircase. Bertie was right behind her. Cornelia had started up the stairs, and Jillian put her hand on the newel post at the end of the banister.

"You stop right there and wait," said Bertie. "Cornelia can take care of this."

"What's going on?" asked Deputy Shaw, who had risen from his chair.

Bertie looked. "She's just gone up to check on the little girl. Did you see her come through here?"

"Yes, she went up, but I haven't seen her come back down. No one's been in or out this door since I've been here."

"And she would have had to walk past us to go out the back,

so she has to be in the house," said Bertie. "I'm sure she's fine, Jillian. Be patient."

Just then, they looked up to see Cornelia coming down quickly, alone. "She's not in Jillian's room or the bathroom. I haven't checked any of the other bedrooms yet, but I just wanted to let you know."

Jillian started up the steps.

"Jillian, stop!" Bertie commanded, but Jillian wasn't listening this time.

Cornelia grabbed Jillian's hand and walked next to her as she went up the steps. Bertie followed behind, ready to catch Jillian if she started to fall backward, as if she—a small eighty-year-old woman—could actually do that.

Their raised voices brought people into the foyer. Victor, Houston, and Chester came out of the library. Patricia, Dorothea, and Kaylee came from the direction of the living room.

"What's going on?" asked Patricia.

"They can't find the little girl," said the deputy. He took out his cell phone and made a call.

Jillian heard Patricia directing Dorothea and Kaylee to check the main level, and told Victor to go guard the back door. She told Houston and Chester to follow her upstairs. Everyone obeyed her instruction as if she were a superior officer.

In the meantime, Jillian, Cornelia, and Bertie had reached the second floor, and Jillian continued to the steps leading to the third floor.

"Where are you going?" asked Bertie.

"The first place I'm checking is the armoire in the attic."

"She wouldn't go in the attic. Not again."

"That's what I thought the first time. I'm going up."

Cornelia and Bertie followed her. Bertie looked over her shoulder as Patricia, Houston, and Chester reached the second floor. "You all check this floor, and we'll check upstairs."

At the top of the stairs on the third floor, they split up. Bertie opened the door to the storage room and called Bonnie's name before going inside. Cornelia walked to Waldon's room, where she began knocking on his door and fairly shouted his name several times. Jillian had reached the attic door, but paused when she heard Houston shout downstairs. The problem was, with the knocking and shouting, she couldn't understand what he said.

She went back to the top of the stairs, and fortunately, Patricia was near there and shouted up, "The door to the balcony was open. Houston's going out to investigate. Chester and I are still checking rooms."

Jillian headed back toward the attic. As soon as she opened the door, she heard Bonnie shouting and pounding on the door of the armoire. She ran to it, and the little girl flung her arms around her neck as soon as she opened the door.

"Gracious, Bonnie. How did you get stuck in here again?"

Bonnie was sobbing and sniffling, but Jillian got the gist of it. "It was . . . that man. He grabbed me and put his hand over my mouth so I couldn't call you, and then he brought me up here and put me in the wardrobe, and I couldn't get out."

Jillian picked up Bonnie and carried her out into the hallway shouting, "I've got her." She heard the shout of "They found her!" repeated several times on the floors below.

Jillian felt a little woozy and her head hurt. She supposed it was a bad idea to lift Bonnie after a concussion, but she'd felt such a surge of adrenaline when she'd found her that she probably could have lifted the whole armoire if needed. Now she sat down on the floor and held Bonnie in her lap, repeating, "It's okay. I've got you," as soothingly as she could, for herself as much as for Bonnie.

Cornelia and Bertie came and stood over her. Jillian heard Cornelia tell Bertie in a low voice, "Waldon's luggage is gone."

Bonnie began to calm down and so did Jillian. "Do you think we can go downstairs now?" Jillian asked.

Bonnie nodded, and they both stood up. They walked downstairs in formation—Bertie leading, Bonnie holding Jillian's hand while Jillian held onto the banister, and Cornelia following behind them.

As they reached the second floor, Houston came in from the balcony to report. Patricia and Chester had been joined by Dorothea, Kaylee, and Victor in the hallway. "I saw it all," Houston said. "They got him. It was a thing of beauty when that officer tackled him and he went down."

"Got who?" asked Patricia.

"Waldon. He was running toward his car even after that cop yelled for him to halt, and when he didn't stop, the cop caught up to him and took him down like he was a toy soldier. I wonder if that boy played football."

Jillian looked down through the balusters to the foyer. "But Deputy Shaw is still downstairs."

"They must have had someone outside they didn't tell us about because he was right on the spot."

"All Waldon's luggage is gone from his room," said Cornelia.

"I found some rope tied to the rail of the balcony down at the end," said Houston, "and there's a pile of luggage down below on the ground. Waldon must have lowered his stuff and then used the same rope to climb down."

Hearing sirens, they all went out to the balcony to watch the events unfold. The sun had set, but the lighting in the front garden provided just enough illumination to see what was going on. Jillian saw Sheriff Henderson pull up first, his headlights brightening the scene even more as he walked across the lawn to where Gooder had Waldon facedown on the ground, handcuffing the older man.

Jillian had to smile. *I guess I finally got my money's worth from my night watchman.*

The next morning, Sheriff Henderson was at Belle Haven fairly early to let everyone know that they were free to go. Jillian was pretty sure they had all already packed. As they gathered once again in the living room—only Aunt Cornelia and Bonnie were absent, as they were in the kitchen—the group's mood was light, a welcome contrast to the previous day. Jillian was glad to see that her remaining guests were free and easy with one another now that there was no suspicion of guilt between them. She thought the search for Bonnie had provided them with a bonding experience that had finally translated to the camaraderie that Dorothea had been hoping for when she first arrived.

Henderson arrived at Belle Haven with a large tote bag that contained the missing children's books, which had been recovered from Waldon Radcliffe's luggage. He took them out of the bag one by one, laying them across the coffee table to let Jillian confirm that they were all there. They were, including *A Little Princess*, which he had been in the process of taking from Jillian's nightstand when Bonnie caught him.

"All of this really had nothing to do with the TV show," said Sheriff Henderson. "It was the books all along. Mrs. Hadley was the intended target of the poisoning because she had realized how valuable a first-edition Beatrix Potter book might be and had discussed it with Radcliffe.

"When I got the call from Deputy Shaw last evening about the little girl being missing, I was already on my way here from the hospital. Mrs. Hadley had regained consciousness and was able to tell us that it was Radcliffe who had drugged her. By the time she realized what was happening she was too out of it to stop him.

"From what we've been able to get from Radcliffe, he rigged Mrs. Hadley's SUV to go into the ravine with her at the wheel and then walked back to Belle Haven. He had just gotten back to the house when he overheard Jillian's phone conversation with Hunter on the front porch. He didn't want her to blow the whistle, so he knocked her out and put her in his trunk. Then he drove to the SUV's location, and dragged, or let her fall, down to the vehicle before putting her inside." He looked at Jillian. "That's how you got all scratched up."

"What about last evening?" asked Chester. "Did you know it was him? How did you know he was going to try to flee?"

"I didn't know it was him at that point, but I knew that whoever it was must have been worried that Mrs. Hadley might regain consciousness and could possibly identify him, so time was running out. I stationed Deputy Jones outside Belle Haven. He was in his patrol car, parked on the road just out of sight. Shaw had called him first to alert him that the little girl was missing, and Gooder was walking toward the house when he saw someone going over the side of the balcony."

"I saw the tackle that took down Waldon," said Houston. "That was a job well done by your man."

Henderson grinned. "Gooder played football in high school."

"I thought he might have."

"At any rate," said Henderson, "Deputy Zane's been at the hospital to keep an eye on Mrs. Hadley, and she asked her about the children's books this morning. That's when we found out that Radcliffe had convinced her to keep quiet about the Potter book. He told her he was going to contact a buyer he knew, and then he said he would tell Jillian after that. We haven't researched it, but from what Radcliffe's told us, the combined value of the books could be in the thousands."

Jillian looked at the stack of books that now spread across the coffee table. "I just can't conceive how someone would attempt murder for these."

"Maybe it didn't start out that way," said Patricia. "Maybe he just wanted to make Avery sick enough to get her out of the house and go home. And if other people were made sick too, it didn't concern him. Then when Florence was poisoned instead, he decided to up the ante to get rid of Avery." She shook her head. "I'm so sorry, everyone. I had no idea when I chose him to be a contestant that he was a . . . a psychopath."

"It wasn't just you who chose him," said Victor. "Houston and I were part of that process as well."

"None of you could have known," said Henderson. "It was just chance that led to all of this. If the books hadn't been part of the equation, your filming probably would have gone off without a hitch."

The small yellow flour-mill booklet floated into Jillian's mind's eye. "Not quite without a hitch. There still would've been Florence to contend with."

"Ah, yes," said Henderson. "How could I forget Mrs. Oglethorpe?"

"Is she still in jail?"

"No. She just spent a few hours there. I let her husband take her to the hotel last night." He looked toward Patricia and Jillian. "Whether she goes back to jail all depends on whether you press charges or not."

"I won't be pressing charges," said Jillian.

Jillian was surprised to hear Patricia say, "Neither will I."

Henderson reached into the tote and took out the yellow booklet and handed it to Jillian. Jillian exchanged a look with Bertie before passing it to Patricia. She accepted it with a nod and mouthed, "Thank you."

"Is anyone going to explain about that book?" asked Kaylee.

Patricia spoke up. "You'll be seeing information about it on my website in the next few days explaining everything. And when the new edition of *Blissful Baking* comes out, to celebrate the fiftieth anniversary of its publication, there will be a biographical section about how my publisher and I used the recipes from this old flour-mill company booklet, or rather one just like it, which I had picked up at the market on Portobello Road during one of our vacations to London in the early 1960s. In the first edition, my publisher didn't want to acknowledge the actual source of the recipes, and after that, we just let it slide. I just hope my fans will forgive me."

Patricia was the last guest to leave Belle Haven, but before she left, she asked Jillian and Bertie if they all might come back in a few weeks, after the other episodes were completed, to finish filming the episode they had begun. "I've spoken to the remaining contestants, and they all agreed to return, with your permission. Even Dorothea."

"Certainly," Bertie replied. "You're a lovely group without Florence and Waldon, and I'd be happy to have you back in my home."

"Thank you, Bertie. And will you continue as regional judge?"

"It would be my genuine pleasure, on one condition."

Patricia looked at the older woman expectantly.

"I want you to ask Dorie Marzette to be the contestant from Alabama in Waldon's place. She's the daughter of my employee, Lenora Ryan, and she's an excellent baker. I'm not quite ready to have another unknown character in this house so soon."

"I don't think anyone can blame you for that," Patricia said solemnly. "I'll talk to her about it. And one more thing."

"Spit it out," Bertie ordered in her usual straightforward manner.

Patricia grinned. "I think you should consider writing a Chocolate Shoppe Bakery cookbook to be published by my publisher."

Bertie opened her mouth, clearly about to decline, but Patricia stopped her. "Please, Bertie, just think about it. Your recipes are amazing. We can discuss it further when I come back."

Jillian was delighted by the idea. She couldn't help but think it might go a long way toward their goal of financial security.

After Jillian said goodbye to Patricia and closed the front door, she leaned her back against it to enjoy the moment. She took a deep breath and felt like the weight of the world had been lifted from her shoulders. She was certain the next go-round with this group in a few weeks would be a piece of cake, at least compared to this session.

As she stood there, Bonnie skipped into the foyer, her shoes clicking on the shiny wooden floor. Since Bonnie had awoken that morning, she seemed to be untarnished by her experience. Jillian had asked if she wanted to talk about it, and they did for a while, ending with Jillian's assurance that "that man" was going to be in prison for a long, long time. She also promised that she would go up to the attic and remove the latch from the armoire as soon as Bertie gave her permission to go up the stairs again. Jillian didn't want to push her luck.

Bonnie stopped skipping when she reached Jillian and took her hand. "Miss Jillian, do you remember when we went to church, and we sat next to Mr. Hunter? He promised we'd have a private talk, but we never got to. Do you think he might come over today before I leave?"

"I don't know, Bonnie. It's a workday, but I'll give him a call and invite him to lunch. Maybe he'll be able to come."

She took out her phone and punched the speed dial for Hunter's number. He answered quickly.

"Hello, Jillian. How are you feeling today?"

"Much better, thank you. I suppose you heard what happened last evening?"

"As a matter of fact, I talked to the sheriff, and he told me everything's been wrapped up there. I know that's a relief for you. Believe me, I feel the same way."

"I called because Bonnie has not forgotten that you agreed to have a private conversation with her before she left." She looked down at Bonnie and winked at her. "If you're able, I thought you might join us for lunch today. Bonnie's mother, grandmother, and great-grandmother are coming over for a visit before Lilith and Bonnie take off for Washington tomorrow."

Hunter paused before answering. "I don't think I can be there for lunch today. I might be able to come over around two thirty this afternoon, but I can't stay long. Would that work?"

"I think so. I know it's been a while since our cousins have been to Belle Haven. I know they'll want to spend as much time as they can with Bertie and Cornelia, so they probably won't be leaving until late afternoon."

"Two thirty it is then."

"One more thing—I wanted to thank you for the lovely flowers you sent." She paused a moment. "And your note." She felt her cheeks warm at the thought of it, aware that Bonnie was watching and listening.

"I meant every word," said Hunter.

They said goodbye, and then Jillian looked at her watch. There was only about an hour left before three generations of her cousins would arrive at Belle Haven to take away the fourth-generation cousin. She and Bonnie hurried to the kitchen where Cornelia had been hard at work preparing a memorable meal for lunchtime. After Patricia left, Bertie had joined Cornelia to help. When Jillian and Bonnie entered the kitchen, they were instructed to set the dining room table.

Jillian found herself especially treasuring the remaining time she had to spend with Bonnie. She tried to teach her the finer points of picking out a tablecloth, napkins, china, and so on to make the table look pleasing. Since Bonnie's mother had already taught her the proper placement for the settings, they finished in a short time. Then Bonnie ran to the kitchen to retrieve the footstool so she could admire their work from a higher perspective.

By the time the cousins arrived, they were all in a situation where they could visit awhile before dinner. Bonnie was over the moon to see her mother again, and the feeling was mutual. She lavished attention on her grandmother and great-grandmother too, asking them questions which they answered with loving patience.

An explanation had to be made about the scratches on Jillian's face, but Jillian tried to keep that to a minimum, thinking she would save the rest of it until she could arrange to talk to Lilith alone.

Genevieve requested a tour of the house so she could revisit memories and to see the redecorating that had occurred since she was last there. She was frail and walked with a cane, so it took a while, but she seemed determined to see all that she could. She had stopped when she first came into the foyer to admire the circular stairs to the stained glass dome above. Jillian thought she would have probably liked to have seen the upstairs again, but the steps were no longer a friendly place for her.

After a leisurely lunch, which included much laughter over the stories Bertie, Cornelia, and Genevieve shared about their youthful escapades when Genevieve came to visit, they settled in the living room where Bertie and Cornelia intended to share the old photographs they had found of Genevieve the previous evening. Genevieve sat down on the sofa and leaned forward to run her hand over the covers of the children's books that were laid out on the coffee table.

"I remember these."

"You do?" asked Jillian.

"Yes, I was little—about Bonnie's age—and I was staying here at Belle Haven with Bertie and Cornelia's mom and dad. This was years before the twins were born. Aunt Nora and Uncle Theo were just newlyweds then. Dad had a small antique shop in Charlotte back in the 1920s, and he went on buying trips to Europe. But that time he wanted to take my mother along too, so they asked if Lonnie and I could stay at Belle Haven.

"While we were here, we both had birthdays. Lonnie was two years older, but both our birthdays were in July. Mine is on the seventh, and his was on the twelfth. Our parents sent us these books as presents. I remember they arrived in a wooden crate, but I can't remember the name of the shop. I thought the street name was funny so I remember that. Back then I thought it was pronounced 'Sharing' Cross Road, but it must have been Charing Cross Road in London, since that's a famous place for bookshops.

"When our parents returned, there was no room to bring the books along in the car, so we left them here. Aunt Nora said she would send them later, but our father died not long after that trip, and we were . . . in disarray, you might say. I think Aunt Nora decided to wait until we remembered and asked for them, but that never happened, and she didn't want to add more to our overwhelming situation. We had to move into an apartment with barely enough room to swing a cat. My mother remarried a couple of years later. I guess we all forgot about the books. I haven't thought about them from that time until now. Where did you find them?"

"The crate was tucked back in a corner of the attic. I only found them a couple of weeks ago. I wondered why they were left up there instead of being in the library."

"Mom must have put them in the attic and had forgotten about them too," Cornelia observed. "Jillian, tell them what we've learned."

Jillian launched into as simple an explanation as she could manage about the events of the past few days to finally get to her point, which was how valuable the books had become. She tried to downplay how dire things had been at times, but that was hard to do. She saw Lilith's eyes widen several times during the course of her story. She hoped that it didn't affect the possibility of Bonnie coming to stay again.

While Jillian was speaking, Bonnie walked over to the coffee table, got down on her knees, and began leafing through the pages of *Peter Pan in Kensington Gardens*. She smiled as she looked at the charming illustrations by Arthur Rackham that denoted it as a first edition, published in 1906. She continued turning the pages until she came across a folded piece of paper tucked into the spine of the book. "What's this?" she asked, handing the paper to Genevieve.

Jillian stopped talking as Genevieve opened the paper with trembling hands. She gazed over the handwritten words on the page. "It's a letter from my parents, dated July 1928." She read it out loud:

Dear Lonnie and Gennie,

Father and I wanted to send you something for your birthdays. We're sorry that these will reach you after your birthdays are already past, but we hope these presents are something you will both be able to enjoy for years to come. We trust you are being good children for your aunt and uncle. We plan to be home by the first part of next month if Father can get passage on the steamer that runs out of Southampton on the 27th. Until then, we love you and miss you.

Love always,

Mother and Father

Even Bonnie was silent for a while after Genevieve finished reading.

Bertie finally asked, "Do you remember the letter?"

Genevieve nodded, her eyes glistening. "I do now, after nearly ninety years. It's hard to believe it could be so long ago."

Cornelia handed her a photo, saying softly, "Look. I knew we had one of your parents."

The older cousins turned their attention back to the photos and began sharing stories about many people who had been long gone, including Genevieve's brother.

The doorbell rang. Jillian hesitated, finding it hard to tear herself away, even though she knew it must be Hunter at the door. It was interesting to hear about family, some of whom she'd met, but knew so little of, and others she hadn't even heard of before. But as it was, she didn't have a chance to move. Bonnie popped up quickly and was already running toward the front door.

"I'll get it! It's Mr. Hunter, and he's coming to see *me*."

"Hunter Greyson is a good friend of the family," Cornelia explained to her cousins. "Bonnie wanted to have a talk with him before she left."

Sure enough, Jillian recognized Hunter's deep voice though she didn't quite catch the words he said. His and Bonnie's voices faded, and Jillian guessed they must have decided to go into the library for their "private talk" right off the bat.

The conversation in the living room continued, and it was several minutes before Bonnie and Hunter entered the living room, both wearing big smiles. Jillian stood up to greet him, and standing next to him, made the introductions. She offered Hunter a seat and a glass of sweet tea, but he apologized, saying that he couldn't stay. He said a general goodbye to all the ladies. However, before leaving the room, he took Jillian's right hand in his and very briefly kissed her on the lips, much to her surprise. When he released Jillian's hand, Bonnie was there to take his, and the winks they exchanged weren't lost on anyone in the room.

"I'll see Mr. Hunter to the door," said Bonnie. The only sound in the room for a full minute was that of Bonnie's shoes as she skipped down the hallway and through the foyer.

"What was that all about?" asked Margaret.

Jillian glanced in the mirror over the fireplace to confirm what she already knew. Her face was a bright pink, which tended to reduce the appearance of the scratches. She took a deep breath before she answered. "Bonnie wanted to have a private conversation with Hunter to determine if he is my boyfriend."

"And is he?"

"I guess I would have to say yes."

She stole a glance at Bertie and Cornelia, who both looked pleased as punch.

When it was nearly time for the cousins to leave, Jillian placed the books that belonged to Genevieve back in the same wooden crate they had been hidden in for so many years, and told Lilith that Bonnie had only two more chapters to go to reach the end of *A Little Princess*. She put that book back on top of the others, just as it had been for all those years.

While the others said their farewells, Jillian borrowed Lilith's keys and carried the crate out to her car with Bonnie at her side. After it was safely in the trunk, they turned to walk back toward the mansion, stopping at almost the same place where they had stood a week and a half ago when Bonnie first set eyes on Belle Haven.

Jillian knelt down to look into Bonnie's eyes. "Bonnie, it has been so lovely having you here. I'm so glad we got to spend time together, and I promise I'll call and write, and come see you in your new house soon." She paused. "And I'll take good care of the dollhouse until you come back to visit again."

"I'm going to miss you, Miss Jillian."

Jillian put her arms around the little girl and hugged her. "I'm going to miss you too, darling."

When they released from the hug, Jillian could tell that there was something else that Bonnie wanted to say, but she seemed to be having a hard time finding the words.

"What is it, honey?"

"I'm going to be so far away, I'm afraid I'll miss it."

"Miss what?"

"Your wedding. When you get married to Mr. Hunter. Will you promise that I can be there?"

Jillian's mouth dropped open. "Sweetheart, Mr. Hunter and I are not planning to get married."

"But he is your boyfriend. Everyone saw him kiss you."

Jillian tried to choose her words carefully. "That doesn't mean we're ready to get married. We're not even engaged."

Bonnie's forehead wrinkled. "What's 'engaged' mean?"

"Well, that's when a man asks a woman if she'd like to get married, and then he gives her a ring, and they promise each other that they will get married. Someday."

Bonnie considered this information. "Then, if you get engaged, and someday get married, do you promise I can be there?"

Jillian tilted her head back and laughed. "Okay. You win. I promise. If I ever get married, you can be my flower girl, or maybe, by that time, a bridesmaid."

The little girl seemed satisfied with that. While they had been talking, the others had come out through the front door of Belle Haven and were saying goodbyes on the veranda. Bonnie ran up the front path and up the stairs to her mother, taking her hand. Though they were still some distance away, Jillian could hear what they were saying.

"Mama, what's a bridesmaid?"

"Umm, that sounds like a question for later," said Lilith. "We can talk about that in the car while we're traveling. Now, Miss Bertie and Miss Cornelia have told me you're welcome to come back any time. Would you like that, dear?"

"Oh yes. I love Miss Bertie and Miss Cornel'a, and especially Miss Jillian."

"It sounds like you had a lot of fun."

"Oh yes," Bonnie repeated. "At Belle Haven, you never know what's going to happen. It's ex'il'rating!"

Half Baked Schemes
Book Eleven Recipe

Here is one of the recipes from *The All-American Baking Contest* at Belle Haven.

Sherry Trifle

Sponge Cake

4 eggs
1 cup sugar
1 teaspoon vanilla

1 cup flour
1 teaspoon baking powder

Custard

2 egg yolks
1½ cups milk
⅓ cup sugar

2 tablespoons cornstarch
⅛ teaspoon salt
2 teaspoons vanilla

Additional

½ to ¾ cup cream (sweet) sherry*
⅓ to ½ cup raspberry jam

Optional: lemon peel, sliced almonds

Topping

1 cup whipping cream

2 tablespoons sugar

*Do not use cooking sherry or wine. Madeira or sweet marsala may be substituted according to personal taste.

Instructions

For sponge cake:

1. Preheat oven to 350 degrees Fahrenheit. Grease and flour a 9-inch round cake pan.

2. Combine eggs, sugar, and vanilla in large bowl and beat with mixer 3 to 4 minutes until sugar is dissolved and mixture is lemon-colored.

3. Combine flour and baking powder; beat into egg mixture, adding one half at a time.

4. Pour mixture into prepared pan.

5. Bake 25 to 30 minutes until toothpick comes out clean. Let rest in pan 10 minutes, then turn out onto rack or plate to allow to cool completely.

For custard:

1. Mix egg yolks and milk together in a glass measuring cup or pitcher.

2. Combine sugar, cornstarch, and salt in a medium saucepan. Slowly whisk milk mixture into dry ingredients. Stirring constantly, cook mixture over medium heat until it thickens and comes to a simmer. Cook 1 minute longer, continuing to stir. Remove from heat and stir in vanilla.

3. Place mixture in bowl. Let cool slightly and then cover surface with cling wrap to prevent skin from forming. Let cool completely.

Assembly:

1. Trim sponge cake to fit and place in bottom of a clear-glass trifle dish or other flat-bottomed dish.

2. Pour sherry over top of cake and allow to soak for a few minutes. Spread a layer of jam over cake. Spread custard over jam layer. Cover with cling wrap and refrigerate.

Topping:

1. Just before serving, place cream and sugar in a cold metal bowl and whisk until stiff peaks form. Pile topping over custard layer.

2. If desired, garnish with lemon peel and sliced almonds.

Up to this point, we've been doing all the writing. Now it's *your* turn!

Tell us what you think about this book, the characters, the bad guy, or anything else you'd like to share with us about this series. We can't wait to hear from *you*!

Log on to give us your feedback at:
https://www.surveymonkey.com/r/ChocolateShoppe

Annie's® FICTION